TOIL AND TROUBLE

An *Olympia Investigations* Novella

SHERRY D. RAMSEY

Ramsey, Sherry D., 1963-, author
Toil and Trouble: An *Olympia Investigations* Novella / Sherry D. Ramsey
Email: sherrydramsey@gmail.com
Web: www.sherrydramsey.com
Cape Breton, Nova Scotia, Canada

Toil and Trouble: An *Olympia Investigations* Novella
Print ISBN: 978-1-7752608-9-9
Ebook ISBN: 978-1-7752608-8-2

DEDICATION

*For my family, all of whom continue to
put up with this whole crazy "writer" thing*

CHAPTER ONE

Oliver knocked on my office door and pushed it open without waiting for me to answer, which he rarely does. His eyes looked wild and his usually-immaculate dark turtleneck and khakis seemed rumpled. I stared. Oliver is my cousin and my assistant, and like me, he can discern and communicate with the supernatural—which would be most of the Olympia Investigations clientele. Unlike me, Oliver is generally poised, calm, and self-assured. It takes a lot to rattle him. He closed the door behind him and leaned against it.

"A...woman to see you," he said, just above a whisper.

"Geez, is she a Medusa or something? You're white as a ghost!"

"Worse. I think she's a witch."

Well, that made some sense. Oliver had endured a bad experience with an urban witch when he was still a teenager, and apparently it was the kind of encounter that can leave a lasting impression. I don't know all the details, because Oliver doesn't talk about it. Most urban witches are friendly, environment-loving, generally benevolent people—but not all.

"What's she doing?" I asked in the same low voice Oliver had used. I didn't think the witch could necessarily hear through walls, but one never knew.

Oliver's lips pressed together in a thin, disapproving line. "Burning incense," he said in a clipped voice. "And using magic, because I can see the aura."

"I'll see her right away," I told him hurriedly. In the witch's mind, she was probably purifying the outer office of Olympia Investigations, but to Oliver this would be akin to an invasion.

Oliver sucked in an audible deep breath and blew it out slowly. Then he opened the door and said to the outer office in a remarkably even tone, "Ms. Sheridan can see you right away."

He stood aside to let the witch enter and I wondered if she noticed, as I did, the way he flinched back ever so slightly as she walked past him.

I stood behind my desk and offered a hand to shake, studying the witch. She looked young, no more than twenty-five or so, although with witches, you could never be sure. A wide blue headband caught her black hair back from her face, although tiny curls escaped around the edges. She carried a red-wine-coloured jacket over one arm and wore a knee-length t-shirt dress in tie-died burgundy and aqua colours. A heavy pendant shaped in an arcane symbol rested in the neckline. Black combat boots and a black suede cross-body bag with a dramatic fringe completed the ensemble. A faint glow of the magic she'd just cast floated around her, almost as if her body gave off pale blue steam. Dark eyes assessed me, and a smile twitched the corners of her mouth as she took my hand. In her other one she held a bundle of smoldering herbs, sweet grey smoke curling lazily up toward the ceiling of my office. Her handshake was cool and firm.

"I'm Acacia Sheridan," I said. "How can I help you?" I sat down again and gestured for her to do the same.

She blew a puff of air onto the smoking herbs and the fire instantly extinguished. She dropped the herbs into her bag and smiled at me. The sweet aroma hung in the air and my habitually bedraggled office felt cleaner and brighter. Urban witches knew their stuff.

"Honore Martel," she offered. She glanced at the door to the outer office and the twitching smile blossomed. "Your assistant seemed a bit...nervous around me." Her speech held a slight French-Canadian accent, although she spoke English with a fluid grace.

"You'll have to excuse Oliver," I told her. "He had a bad experience with a witch long ago and it left him...wary. It's nothing personal."

"Ah." Honore Martel didn't ask, *wary of what?* She wouldn't be here, after all, if she didn't know of my ability to deal with the supernatural. And after the burning herbs and accompanying cantrip, she probably felt it was obvious to me what she was. Witches are human (although not, of course, exclusively), so it's not something Oliver and I can automatically sense upon meeting one. But as soon as they cast a spell or perform magic, the aura of that energy use makes it abundantly clear.

"I—we—would like to hire your services," she said, letting the topic of Oliver go. "You are adept at finding things that have gone missing?"

"I have a certain amount of experience," I said cautiously. "Who is 'we'? And what have you lost?"

Honore sat back more comfortably in the big blue armchair across from my desk and crossed her arms, the fingers of one hand tapping on the other bicep.

"'We' are myself and my six sisters—coven sisters, that is," she clarified. My eyes might have gone a little wide at the idea of seven sisters in one family. Being an only child myself, that notion was far outside the realm of my own experience. But I knew urban witches often gathered in tribes or small groups and weren't averse to using the traditional word—*coven*—to describe themselves. I nodded for her to continue.

"We recently tried—" she halted, then sighed and began again. "We—made a mistake. We wanted to summon a benevolent spirit to cleanse and purify a former crack house over on Cooke Street."

I felt my eyebrows lift. "Okay."

"A local housing co-op for at-risk youth bought the place after the police cleaned out the dealers, and the city put it up for tax sale. Blanche—one of my sisters—knows the coordinator and offered our help to freshen up the place. We helped them clean and paint and put down new floors, and then we thought this ritual would be the finishing touch."

I have to admit, inside I was laughing at Oliver. He was afraid of an urban witch who helped create safe homes for at-risk youth? But I didn't let my amusement show on my face. It was clear from Honore's voice that the bad part of the story was still to come.

"What went wrong?"

She licked her lips. "The spirit that appeared in answer to the ritual—it wasn't benevolent. It was—" she swallowed and closed her eyes for a breath, "quite the opposite. It broke free of the summoning circle and attacked Chloe, then disappeared. She's still in the hospital." The smile from earlier was gone now, as if it had never been.

I didn't feel like laughing any more, either. "That's terrible. But can't you call it back, or banish it, or something? I don't know much about the Practice, but if you summoned it—"

The young witch shook her head. "Without Chloe, we're not strong enough. She was the ritual's keystone, and it's—well, it's complicated. It's not so easy to just stick someone in her place. I don't know how long she'll be in the hospital."

"Could you get someone else to help? Sort of— borrow a witch from another coven? You can't be the only ones in the city."

Honore's dark eyes looked tired. "We'd really like to fix this without too many other practitioners knowing. It won't be easy to convince someone to stand in the keystone position if they know what happened, either. It could be dangerous. We'd need someone very experienced, and there can be...friction, between covens."

I pulled a deep breath and sighed. "All right. But what do you want me to do? I can communicate with a lot of creatures, but I don't have any real ability beyond that. And I'm definitely not a practitioner."

The young witch nodded. "I know. We're hoping you can help track him down, because he's doing something to hide from us. I've been scrying him for two days now and all I get are glimpses, but he's gone before we can reach him."

I really didn't like the way this was going. "What do you plan to do if you find him? And by the way, you haven't told me what 'he' really is, yet."

"We think if we can find him and get close, we can put a geas on him until Chloe's better and we can send him back for good. But when we do get a read on him, we can't get there quickly enough. We thought you might do better at tracking him down, because you'll be able to identify him just by looking."

I stared at my slightly scarred and battered desk, thinking. "With enough information I might be able to," I admitted. I looked up and caught her gaze. "I mean, I have to know where to look. And you'll have to tell me everything before I agree."

Honore matched my sigh. "That's the tricky part," she said slowly. "It's—he's—we're pretty sure he's a demon. And it's only a matter of time before he starts doing what demons loose on Earth do."

I sat back in my chair as if she'd pushed me. "You mean killing people."

The young urban witch nodded, and her brown

eyes reflected the fear I knew showed in my own.

After we'd arranged to meet with the rest of the coven the next day and Honore had left, I went out to reception to talk to Oliver. The lemony smell of cleaner scented the air, erasing the witch's sweet incense. That meant Oliver was scrubbing down the tiny kitchen area in the outer office, even though it was one of the few places in the office that was usually spotless. I sat in his chair behind the reception desk. He'd managed to get me to pay for a new chair a few weeks ago, and I realized now how much nicer it was than mine. I might have to do something about that with the funds from the witches' fees. I put my feet up on the desk. Usually Oliver hates that, but this time he didn't say a word. He didn't even look over at me.

"When you finish cleaning the coffee maker, you should put on another pot," I suggested as the hot water began bubbling and snorting and the sharp tang of vinegar filled the air. When Oliver cleans—especially if it's anxiety cleaning—he goes all out. He'd pushed up the sleeves of his charcoal turtleneck and everything. This was serious.

"Are you working for her?" he asked, neatly tying off a compost bag of used coffee grounds.

I noticed he said *you*, not *we*. Not a good sign.

"She seems very nice," I told him. "Her coven helps at-risk youth find safe places to live."

He eyed me silently over the coffee maker as the diluted vinegar and water perked its way through the inner workings, spiking the air. "So you *are* working for her. May I request a leave of absence?"

"Of course you may. And I'll consider it. But I think I might need your help with this one, Oliver."

He scrubbed vigorously at a spot—probably invisible—on the tiny countertop for a moment, then turned and shook the cleaning cloth at me. "How many times have I asked to go along with you on a case?"

"Lots, and sometimes—"

"*Sometimes* you let me go. And now there's a case with a witch for a client—"

"To be precise, there are seven of them in the coven—"

"So there's a case involving multiple witches—*witches*—and THIS is the one where you need my help?" He dropped the cloth and leaned back against the counter, crossing his arms and glaring at me.

I swallowed. "I'm sorry? Look, I know what happened to you was—"

"No." He held up a hand to stop me. "We're not talking about that."

I let my feet drop back to the floor, leaning forward

in the chair and speaking quickly. "Okay. Here's the thing. They accidentally summoned a demon, and they need help to find him before he starts killing people. You and I—well, we're uniquely qualified to do that, aren't we?"

Oliver's glare turned into a disbelieving stare as his eyes went wide. "*Accidentally*? Summoned a demon?" He gave a short bark of laughter that held no real amusement. "How inept can they be?"

That made me squirm a little, because I'd had the same thought. But Honore Martel had seemed so earnest and troubled that I'd let it slide. "I know it sounds bad, but mistakes happen. Accidents happen. We don't have all the details yet. And I think the important thing here is: there's a demon loose."

Now Oliver turned away from me, deliberately staring at an empty chair in the waiting area. He opened his mouth and closed it again. "We haven't dealt with a demon before," he said finally.

I shook my head. "Closest I've ever come were those stories Nonna Pia used to tell." Our grandmother Olympia, for whom I'd named the agency, had passed on the dubious gift of communing with the supernatural, and she'd lived an interesting life herself because of it.

Oliver sighed. "And they were bad. Really bad." He

met my gaze again, and I thought some of the anger had dissipated. "You really think they're 'good' witches?"

He didn't add *if such a thing really exists*, but I heard it in his tone. I shrugged. "They sound like it. I'll make you a promise, okay? They do anything, or we even hear of them doing anything, that makes you uncomfortable, you can walk away."

Oliver picked up the cleaning cloth from the counter and wordlessly wiped down the side of the coffee maker. It had stopped its muttering and sputtering, and the scent of warm vinegar filled the air. I had to admit it felt cleansing. But I was ready for it to smell like coffee again.

"Anything at all," I reiterated. "Just give it a try?"

"All right," he said finally. "I guess we're going demon hunting. I hate it when you're reasonable." And he threw the cloth at me.

I caught it and smiled. "I have my moments."

"And I have to go and get ready to talk to witches," he said in a grim voice. "I have some things to do, so you'll have to make your own coffee. I'll see you in the morning."

CHAPTER TWO

Oliver arrived for work late, which never happens. I let it slide, though, because I saw what he'd meant by "getting ready" to deal with witches. It threw me a little. He wore a light grey flight jacket I'd never seen before, with a row of colourful embroidered sigils running down the left side, over his heart to the hem. An amulet shaped like a stylized dog nestled under the collar of his turtleneck, suspended from a leather strip. And on the middle finger of his left hand a wide aluminum band glowed dully in the office lights.

I raised an eyebrow. "What's all this?"

"Protection," Oliver said briefly.

"Did you bring anything for me?"

"You don't think you need it."

I made a point of looking at his various "protections." "Well, I didn't, but now you're making me wonder. Are these for protection against the witches, or the demon?"

Oliver shrugged. "Both, I hope."

"I'm going after the demon, too."

He sighed. "True enough." He slipped the ring off his finger and held it out to me. "This might have been overkill, anyway. Just don't lose it."

The band was too big to fit anything but my thumb, but I slid it on. "What does it do?"

"Gives you a plus one to Constitution," he said with the first smile he'd offered all morning.

"Great, I'll make sure the DM knows I have it the next time I play Dungeons and Dragons."

"Makes you more difficult to injure with a physical attack," Oliver said, relenting. He touched the dog-shaped amulet at this throat. "But this one does the same thing. That's why I said maybe the ring was overkill."

"All right, let's put the *Back Soon* sign on the door and go talk to some witches," I said, and Oliver grimaced but followed me out of the office.

Honore Martel had given me an address over on Riverview Road, which turned out to be an older warehouse-type building with a small storefront on the street side. The sign on the facade read "Seven Sisters Health & Beauty", and the window displayed brightly-coloured creams and lotions, and pyramid stacks of soaps and bath bombs. Notes proclaimed that all the products were made on-site and used only "natural" ingredients.

I checked the address against Honore's, and it matched all right. "This must be the place," I told Oliver. "Not too sinister-looking, right?"

He gave me a look that served as an unprintable answer, and we pushed the door open and stepped inside. A tinkling chime announced our arrival.

The riot of scents hit us the moment the door opened: vanilla, lavender, coconut, patchouli, eucalyptus, and too many others to tease apart. Two women, one younger and one in her thirties, were busy creating an intricate and precariously-balanced structure of tiny soaps, but looked up with smiles as we entered. Neither of them was Honore. White-painted shelves lined the shop walls, holding bottles and jars filled with colourful potions and creams. Bunches of drying herbs and flowers hung from the rafters, interspersed with sparkling crystals that caught the morning light and tossed rainbows around the room.

"Is Honore around?" I asked one of the women. She had flawless skin the colour of my darkest-ever tan and a smile that felt like the sun coming out. She brushed soap residue on her bright yellow apron and came forward to shake my hand. Her grip was brief but friendly and confident, and a lemon-vanilla scent wafted with her.

"She's in the wardroom," she said, offering Oliver her hand in turn. "I'm Sasha, and this is Gennai. I'll take you to Honore."

Despite whatever might be happening in Oliver's mind and heart, he shook Shasha's hand with good grace and no hesitation. The other woman lifted a hand in greeting but didn't take the other off the half-finished soap stack. We followed Sasha through a narrow door at the back of the shop and I gave Oliver an encouraging smile. He offered me a glare in return and I guessed he hadn't felt quite the same warmth from Sasha as I had. But then I'm a sucker for vanilla.

The room we entered resembled an industrial kitchen, lined with oversized appliances and stainless-steel shelving. The cozy homeness of the outer shop was replaced by a feeling of brisk efficiency. This impression was helped along by the three women—presumably three more of Honore's coven—who moved around in the room. A short, thick-waisted woman with her silver-threaded hair tied back in a Hello Kitty bandanna stirred a rich-scented mixture bubbling in an enormous pot on the stove. A slim woman with blond-highlighted hair and more piercings than I could count looked up from measuring ingredients into an array of multicoloured ramekins precisely lined up on the counter. She smiled and nodded as we followed Sasha through the kitchen. The third woman, taller than Oliver and made even taller by the gloriously messy pile of auburn hair piled atop her head, left the notebook she'd been writing in and joined us.

"I'm Jo," she said in a warm, husky voice with a slight accent I couldn't quite place. "You're the detectives?"

"Yes," I told her. "I hope we'll be able to help out."

"So do I," she said, worry lines crinkling around her eyes.

Another door led out of the kitchen and we finally arrived in the wardroom. I hadn't been sure what the term meant, although as I stepped inside I realized this was where the coven did their actual magic. It permeated the room, and my supernatural sense picked up overlays of bright, multicoloured auras tracing the walls, floors, and every surface. It was so strong it manifested as a scent as well, similar to the storefront but underlaid with metallic and earthen notes. Oliver hesitated on the threshold and then stepped inside. I saw his hands clench into fists and release a couple of times, so his senses must be jangling, too.

"Just breathe," I whispered to him. "It's going to be

fine."

"It may be fine, but no place like this is *safe*," Oliver hissed back.

This room was larger than the kitchen, probably taking up two-thirds of the warehouse area. Brick walls and a soaring ceiling studded with hanging light fixtures defined the space. A huge, beautifully intricate mandala mosaic filled the centre of the floor with a riot of colourful ceramic and glass shards—no nasty pentacles for these women, apparently. The circle's bright design was marred by one long streak of black, like soot or grease, running from the centre to one side. A long credenza sat against one wall, holding two laptops and a couple of tablets with dangling charging cords. Drying herbs and flowers festooned the far wall, adding to the rich floral and spicy entanglement of aromas. Someone had pinned botanical drawings chalked in a firm but sure hand to the wall above the credenza.

My nose was just registering something amiss, a dank chemical odor that felt wrong, when Honore rose from a seat at a long, boardroom-style table to our left, and came forward with a smile. She shook my hand but didn't offer hers to Oliver, favouring him with a smile and a nod instead. She obviously remembered his reaction to her in my office.

"Thank you so much for coming," she said. She hissed a long exhale out between her teeth, opening her arms to encompass the room. "This is where it happened."

I nodded toward the mandala. "I guess that's the explanation for the mark over there?"

Her bright eyes darkened as her brows drew down. She nodded, biting her lower lip, then led us over to the circle, stopping just outside the edge.

"We were at our usual stations around the edge for the summoning. Chloe stood there." Honore pointed to the spot outside the rim of the circle where the dark streak ended in an ugly blotch, as if someone had dropped a pouch of gunpowder and it had burst on contact.

Measuring with my eyes, I thought the mandala must be about twenty feet across. The central design spiraled out to seven distinct mosaic rosettes spaced evenly around the circle's edge. I imagined the seven witches standing, each on a rosette, around the perimeter of the mandala to perform their rites. Some eight feet separated one rosette from the next. The thing was enormous. I wrenched my attention back to Honore.

"We finished the incantation and the demon appeared in the inner circle," she said, now stepping into the mandala and walking to the centre. I followed her, cautiously avoiding the sooty streak marring the colours. Oliver didn't follow us.

I knelt to brush fingertips across the intricate surface. The main area of the floor was poured and polished concrete, and the mosaic had been inset. It felt cool to the touch. There was, indeed, an inner circle about three feet across, scribed by three concentric lines; one white, one black, and one green. Honore knelt beside me.

"It—he—shouldn't have been able to cross these three lines, let alone leave the mandala," she said. "I still don't understand what happened."

"And he went straight for Chloe?"

Honore pointed to the black mar across the circle. "As you can see. As the keystone, she should have been the best-protected of all of us."

I pursed my lips, thinking. "What else can you tell us about the summoning?"

Honore stood, not meeting my eyes. "I can't disclose particulars to someone not of the Practice."

"No, of course not." I stood, too. "I meant in general. Did it go smoothly? Did anything unusual happen, during the ritual, or before it?"

"Chloe said her battery was low," Jo said in her husky voice from the other side of the room.

I looked to see her holding one of the tablets from the credenza. This one wasn't plugged in, and I crossed to her. The tablet's screen was marred by a spiderweb crack, as if a bullet had struck it in the centre. She turned it over, so I could see its back also bore a sooty black scar.

"I'm not...you use electronic tablets in your rituals?"

Jo smiled. "We're a very modern coven, Acacia."

I felt a little off-balance. "Okay, but I'm still not sure..."

Jo shrugged. "The Practicing community is pretty strong on the Internet. We share spells, rituals, plan events. We source ingredients for the shop and our rites."

Honore joined us, and even Oliver had unbent enough—or his curiosity finally got the better of him once technology was involved—to peer over my shoulder at the ruined tablet.

"We also draw some of the energy for rituals this way," Honore said. Jo shot her a glance, but the other woman shrugged. "They have to know at least a little bit to be able to help us."

Jo sighed. "I suppose."

"Witches have always drawn most of what you might call our 'spell energy' from our own reserves, and our connection to the world around us," Honore explained. "And, I won't deny it, some darker Practitioners have tapped into the energy of other people, willing or not."

I felt Oliver twitch behind me, and then go very, very still.

"That's the dark side of the Practice; we don't approve of it or practice in that way," Jo said, her voice solemn.

Honore smiled, breaking a tension that had formed, invisibly, around us. "But the Internet is what you might call a gold mine of excess energy."

"How so?" Oliver asked. I was surprised to hear him speak, and his voice sounded calm.

"So many people pouring their energy into so many things on the Internet," Jo said. "Sometimes more energy than is actually needed to accomplish what they want to do. So much passion, so much enthusiasm! Think about it. The energy you can tap into from cat videos alone..." She grinned.

For a heartbeat I thought she was joking, but I realized she meant it. Oliver stepped around beside me and held out a hand for the tablet. Jo passed it to him and he turned it over in his hands. He ran a thoughtful finger over the cracked screen.

"So at least some portion of your spells run on

Internet energy," he mused. "That could be significant."

I turned to him with a frown. "What do you mean?"

He looked up and met my eyes. "There's a lot of dark stuff on the Internet."

"You think they tapped into—what? A virus or something?"

"Or something. Maybe." Oliver turned to Honore, addressing her directly for the first time. "You don't have to go into detail about your ritual, just describe what happened when things went wrong."

She looked down at the mandala for a moment, as if gathering her thoughts. "We finished the summoning, and the spirit began to coalesce inside the inner circle. At that point, Chloe was about to instruct him on what we wanted him to do, the parameters of the geas—"

"That's basically the boundaries the summoned spirit has to operate within," Jo interjected.

I nodded and Honore continued. "And how long we would keep him on this plane. But she didn't get that far." Sudden tears glistened in Honore's eyes. "There was a terrible smell—that's what I noticed first—the first clue that something was wrong. As he formed more fully, I realized we had the wrong kind of spirit. And then he just *looked* at Chloe. Caught her eyes when she glanced up from her tablet. She seemed sort of—frozen. And then he moved toward her so fast. It was just a streak of movement."

"He just—collided with her." Jo took up the story. "I heard the tablet crack—she dropped it, but I heard the crack before it hit the floor. A flash of light so bright I closed my eyes without thinking about it. When I opened them, Chloe was unconscious on the floor, and the demon was gone."

"Can we speak to Chloe?" I asked. "How is she doing?"

Honore and Jo shared a glance, and Honore shook her head. "I don't think she should have visitors just yet. This was really a terrible experience for her."

"All right. And you're sure he's still here? Like, on this plane?" I asked. It sounded as if no-one had seen the demon leave the wardroom. "Maybe when it broke the circle, that negated the summoning. Is it possible the bright light was the demon being—I don't know, sucked back to its original plane of existence?"

Honore gave a soft, humourless chuckle. "I wish I could believe that. But remember, our scrying has located him here, in the city. He simply disappears before we can get to where we find him. No, I'm afraid he's definitely here."

"Right. Okay." I looked at Oliver, wondering if he

had any more questions, but he was staring down at the tablet he still held. He'd picked another one up off the credenza and seemed to be comparing the two devices. "Well, we'll see what we can do. I don't suppose you have description of him?"

Honore and Jo looked at each other, then shook their heads. "It all happened so fast," Jo said. "He'd barely fully apparated before he moved. And after all, he's a demon. He can change his appearance every day if he wants."

"Oh, right." I nodded as if this wasn't new information to me.

"But you should be able to sense him if you get near enough, isn't that right?" Honore asked me anxiously. "I thought that was sort of your thing."

"Sure, it is," I reassured her. It was true, Oliver and I could both sense supernatural creatures in our vicinity, even those other humans couldn't see, hear, or sense. We'd know the demon when we saw him, although I didn't know precisely what would tip us off. I'd recently worked for a vampire—her tell was a coppery taste like blood in the back of my throat and a shadow over like like a great pair of wings. All supernaturals had something. But although ours was a small city, it was still a city. It definitely would have helped to have a description of who we'd be hunting.

"All right, I guess that's all we need for now. We'll let you both get back to work. We'll be in touch."

Outside the front door of Seven Sisters Health & Beauty, I took a deep lungful of fresh autumn air. Well, city air, but at least it was outdoors. The heavily scented interior of the warehouse had seemed pleasant at first, but began to cloy after a while, particularly when the scents of magic and a demonic presence had entered the mix.

I turned to Oliver. "Well, what do you think?"

"Witches," he snorted. "Find a witch, find trouble." And he stalked off toward the car. I followed him. I sort of had to agree.

Back at the office of Olympia Investigations, I sat behind my desk and opened my laptop while Oliver set coffee brewing. The mouth-watering scent helped clear the last of the warehouse smells from my nose, including the dank aroma of the demon. "Maybe we should borrow a dog and see if we could track the demon by scent," I called to Oliver out in reception.

He came in with two steaming mugs. "I don't know how you'd get a dog to zero in on the demon smell, though," he said. "Too much competition in that warehouse."

I took my coffee and sipped it. Heaven. "I was half-joking," I told him. "I don't know anything about dogs."

Oliver left my office and came back with his own laptop under his arm. He set it on the opposite side of my desk and opened it, then pulled one of the big blue armchairs closer to my desk and sat. "I actually have a friend who breeds beagles," he said. "But I'd rather not draw her into this."

I looked at him speculatively for a moment. I knew nothing of this friend. Now wasn't the time to delve into Oliver's personal life, though. "All right. How do we tackle this?"

Oliver leaned back in his chair and cradled his coffee mug in both hands. "Roaming around the city hoping to stumble across him seems ineffective. It's not like we have long-range radar to find him—we have to at least get close first. I was thinking we should look online and research the accumulated wisdom on demons. What they like, where they go, what they do when they're on this plane."

"Yeah, that doesn't sound like an Internet rabbit hole at all. Also, I'm not keen on becoming an expert on demonic pastimes."

"I think if we stick to the 'official' channels the witches use, we'll be more likely to find something useful."

"And we find those, how?"

Oliver grinned. "One of those working tablets might have turned on when I picked it up. And I might have noticed a few things on it while the witches were explaining what happened at the summoning."

My mouth dropped open a bit and I felt my eyes go wide. "You went behind our clients' backs? You snooped on their tablet?"

Oliver shrugged. "It wasn't even password protected. Witches are secretive about the Practice, but how are we supposed to help them if they keep us in the dark?" He sketched an "x" over the left side of his chest with an index finger. "I promise I won't be drawn into the dark side of witchcraft."

"But what about me? What if I succumb to the lure of Dark Practice?"

"Some might argue you're already a witch, or some word that's very similar," Oliver said with a grin. "Now, type in this URL and let's get to work."

Half an hour and a second cup of coffee later, Oliver said, "Huh."

I looked up. "What?" We'd accessed a lot of Practitioner web pages, chat rooms, and article repositories from the starting points Oliver had collected, but hadn't found a whole lot yet that I thought would help us track down the demon. I was learning a lot more about modern witchcraft than I'd previously known, however. I was seriously considering asking for a charm to keep socks from slipping and underwear from riding up as part of the payment for this case. Who knew such wonders existed?

Oliver tapped a finger against his lips. "I wonder if Chloe might have been keeping secrets from her coven sisters?"

"What do you mean?"

Oliver read from the screen. "*A minimum of six months should be allowed to pass between summonings where a Practitioner stands in the keystone position. Binding entanglements between Practitioner and Summoned Spirit may persist this long, making it impossible for the Practitioner to summon any other spirit successfully. Stronger spirits may even exploit these connections and appear instead of an intended spirit, endangering the Practitioner and causing unpredictable results.*"

"Hmm." I mulled that over. "So you're thinking if Chloe had summoned *this* demon before, sometime in the last six months, her connection to him might have pulled him in by mistake."

"I'd say the results qualify as 'unpredictable.' And the other witches might not have known she had that connection. I wonder how long she's been a part of this coven?"

"Or," I continued to muse, "it might not have been a mistake. Chloe should have known about the six-month waiting period. I mean, if we could find this information in half an hour, she must have known."

Oliver nodded. "Yeah. Maybe she meant to summon this guy all along."

"But why would she do that? And not tell the others? And why would he attack her immediately?"

"I don't know. But maybe we need to talk to Chloe."

I pursed my lips. "And the other witches didn't seem to want us to do that."

Oliver met my eyes. There was a bit of a challenge in them, I thought. "Do we do it anyway?"

I nodded. "I think maybe we do."

CHAPTER THREE

There was only one major medical centre in our small city, supported by a few walk-in clinics, so it wasn't hard to figure out where Chloe would be. I didn't want to alert Honore and the others that we planned to go talk to their coven sister, but Oliver looked up the business information for Seven Sisters Health & Beauty and found Chloe's full name on the list of partners. I tease Oliver a lot, but he's darn good at ferreting out information, and he knows where to look for things.

We pushed through the doors of Healing Sisters Hospital, grateful to leave the chill wind of the parking lot behind, and stopped at the front desk. Oliver carried a spray of lavender and pot marigolds, both known for their healing properties. Our thinking was that we might as well put our best foot forward with the injured witch. I asked the receptionist where we might find Chloe August, and she looked up a room number on her computer screen. We headed for the elevator to the fourth floor.

"That was easy," I said to Oliver as we glided upwards in the metal box. "Now, as long as none of the other witches are here..."

"They were all at the warehouse earlier," Oliver said. "They're probably shorthanded without her, so they won't be visiting around the clock."

We went unchallenged in the hospital hallways, since this was the middle of afternoon visiting hours and the corridors bustled with medical staff and other visitors. The door to Chloe's room stood slightly ajar as we approached, and all was quiet within. Without knocking, I pushed it open enough to see inside. A woman with tangled, sweat-dampened blonde hair lay on the single white-sheeted bed, apparently asleep. The room appeared empty of anyone else, so Oliver and I moved quietly inside.

As I got a better look at Chloe August, I saw more of the results of the summoning-gone-wrong. Her left hand, presumably the one in which she'd been holding the tablet, was heavily bandaged. Her face looked bruised, particularly underneath her closed eyes, as if she'd been in a fistfight and emerged with two shiners. Another large, square bandage covered her forehead, held in place with transparent medical tape. Her breathing rasped in and out, catchy and uneven, not the smooth breaths of a sound sleeper. A monitor beeped softly and rhythmically in the background.

I put a tentative hand out to touch her, but before I made contact she mumbled something I couldn't hear, and jerked her head to the side. I jumped back, startled, bumping into Oliver who almost dropped the flowers.

"Geez, Acacia," he whispered. "Who's the one afraid of witches, here?" He set the flowers on the small stand next to the bed.

I ignored him and collected myself, then put a hand on Chloe's arm. Her skin felt feverish and damp. "Chloe?" I said in a quiet voice. "We'd like to ask you some questions about your...accident."

I expected Chloe's eyes to flutter open, but she didn't appear to wake. Instead, she twitched her arm away from my touch as if it burned her, and threw her head to the other side.

She muttered something, a single syllable. Almost "no," but accented somehow. When she repeated it, I realized it was *"Non."* 'No,' but in French. She spoke again, but her words were too low and quick for me to catch. I glanced at Oliver.

"What did she say? You've still got your French from high school, right?"

Oliver raised both eyebrows at me. "Wow, you don't expect much. I can still read some French, but catching it in conversation is a lot trickier. I might pick up a word or two—"

"Then come closer and see if you can get anything she says!"

Obediently, although with a huff of annoyance, Oliver stepped up beside me and leaned closer to Chloe. Whatever she'd said a few seconds ago, she repeated, although with more agitation. At least it sounded the same to me. I looked the question at Oliver. He grimaced.

"...*ne me contrôleras pas...*" he said. "I think. Something about 'won't control me,' or maybe 'don't control me.'"

"She might mean the demon," I whispered.

Oliver shrugged and leaned over Chloe again. Her right hand had moved to pluck lightly at the tape securing an IV tube in the back of her left. "*L'enlever,*" she whispered. "*L'enlever.*"

"I think she wants the IV out?" Oliver said doubtfully. "She might not be talking about the demon at all. Maybe she doesn't like all this medical intrusion."

I put a gentle hand on her fretful one and guided it away from the IV tape. If she was going to pull that thing out, I didn't want to be here for it. I had visions of fountaining spurts of blood, although I knew that was probably overdramatic. The beeping monitor had increased its cadence, and the insistent sound was making me feel oddly nauseated. I tried again to get through to her, raising my voice slightly.

"Chloe, I'm trying to help Honore and your sisters. Can you tell me anything about why the summoning went wrong?"

This time the reaction was swift. She stiffened, and then her right hand swung in an arc across her body, her palm catching me squarely on the cheek with a sharp slap. "*Sortez!*" she hissed. "*Sortez!* Get out!" Her eyes remained closed, but the malevolence in her words hit me like a second slap. She lifted both hands and began twisting them in arcane gestures, intoning words I couldn't parse. This was no longer French, but something older, stranger, and infused with an almost tangible power.

I was still in shock from the slap, but I felt Oliver grab my upper arms and pull me back from the bedside. "She's casting a spell! We have to get out of here."

He'd begun to propel me toward the door, but I recovered my senses and made it there without his urging. It didn't take Oliver's paranoia to know that a barely-conscious witch casting an unknown spell was not something to stick around for. I had a thought that she might not be able to cast successfully with her bandaged hand, but it wasn't worth the risk to stay and find out. We slipped back into the hall and pulled the door almost shut, trying to appear casual as we stepped away. A crash—or maybe a small explosion—came from the room behind us. With a glance at each other we quickened our pace. Then the scream emerged from Chloe's room, a thin, high-pitched wail that soared over hallway chatter and beeping medical devices. A nurse emerged from a station further up the hall and hurried toward Chloe's room as we stopped and stared around like everyone else for camouflage. Once the nurse had passed us, we beelined for the stairwell, not willing to wait for the elevator.

I felt like I didn't start breathing again until we opened the doors and the cold wind hit my face. I turned to Oliver. His skin was so ashen I almost made him go back into the hospital. But as I looked at him, he reached up and touched the amulet around his neck, and it seemed to calm him. I rubbed a finger across the ring he'd loaned me, wishing it would make me feel better.

"What the heck just happened?" I demanded.

Oliver shook his head. "No idea. But I think I know

why the witches didn't want us to come and see her."
We walked briskly toward the car, which we'd had to
leave at the very end of the parking lot. There never
seemed to be an empty space near the doors unless you
arrived at 5 a.m.

I put a hand to my cheek, where the witch's slap
still burned. I could practically feel where her fingers
had made long, red imprints on my skin. "We still need
more information. And I have a feeling the six other
sisters have been as forthcoming as they're likely to be
unless we press them."

Oliver opened his mouth to say something, but the
words didn't make it out. He felt it at the same time I
did, and we both stopped walking despite the desire to
get out of the cold. We should have kept moving, but
the sensations were too strong to ignore. A strong
chemical smell like smoldering plastic itched in my
nose, accompanied by a ripple of ominously dark
energy.

The presence of the demon.

I shot a hand out as unobtrusively as I could and caught
the sleeve of Oliver's flight jacket before he could react.
"Don't move," I hissed. "Don't look around. We don't
want him to know he's been spotted, right? Pretend we
just stopped to talk."

Oliver hitched a deep breath. "Right. In the middle of a freezing parking lot. That'll be believable."

"It'll just be for a minute while we figure out what to do."

"I assume you have the witches on speed dial?"

I twisted a rueful half-smile. "Didn't think I needed to do that just yet, since we hadn't even started searching," I said. "But I can try to call Honore. I'll do it casually. We'll have to play this by ear and see what he's up to. Try to look like we're just carrying on our conversation before we part ways."

Oliver patted my hand as if I'd been holding his arm in a comforting way. "Yes. We just came out from visiting a family member in the hospital, and we're talking about them. Okay, where do you think the demon is? Can you see him?"

The hospital was behind me, so I scanned the parking lot beyond Oliver and to both sides, as far as I could with my peripheral vision. "Nobody moving in the lot as far as I can see."

Oliver was half-turned sideways to the hospital. "There's a couple on a bench—the woman is in a hospital gown and the guy is having a cigarette. I'm pretty sure they were there when we walked out, and I didn't sense anything. There's a nurse walking toward her car, talking on a cell phone. That's all I see in this direction."

"Okay. I'm going to keep talking to you and just turn casually to see the other side..." I did so, and spotted a lone man walking toward the hospital's front doors. I glanced away quickly, looking back at Oliver's face. I smiled and nodded as if he'd just said something encouraging. "Bingo. He's headed into the hospital," I hissed between my teeth. "Dark hair, denim jacket, cowboy boots. I mean, that seems so stereotypical for a demon, somehow."

Oliver smiled but didn't laugh. "Think he's trying to get to Chloe?"

I shoved my hands in my pockets and shrugged. "I don't know why else he'd be here." I pulled out my cell phone and scrolled through numbers, tapping the one for Honore when I found it. I put the phone to my ear and the wide ring on my thumb clinked against the case. It was an oddly comforting reminder of Oliver's "precautions."

"Is it ringing?" Oliver asked. "I feel like I have a bull's-eye painted on my back. He must be looking straight at us."

"Calm down, people stand around outside and talk all the time, and I don't want to make it obvious that I'm turning to look at him again," I told him, but I was willing Honore to answer her phone quickly.

"Did he go inside yet? Just glance over."

I risked it. The man had stopped just before the entrance doors and stood staring straight at us. The burning plastic smell hadn't left the air, and now I saw that his face was limned with reddish light, as if a penlight with a coloured filter illuminated it. Scattered, shifting runnels of black traced his skin. I assumed these weren't visible to other humans, or it would have drawn some reaction from the couple near the hospital doors.

I half-smiled and looked back to Oliver. "Shit, he's looking this way. Do not look over there."

"The guy on the bench just butted out his cigarette and he and the woman are heading back inside," Oliver observed. "The nurse just got in her car."

I heard the engine turn over, and seconds later the crunch of wheels on gravel. Unless someone else appeared, we were about to be alone in the parking lot with the demon. And he seemed unusually interested in us.

"Hello?" Honore's voice on the phone was the best thing I'd ever heard.

"We're at the hospital," I said, smiling and nodding at Oliver, "outside, in the parking lot. I think your guy is here."

"*Mon Dieu,*" she whispered. "Is he after Chloe?"

"Well I don't think he's here for bloodwork," I said tightly. "Can you get here fast?"

The reassuring words I was hoping for didn't come. Instead there was a silence that seemed far too long. "I'm not with the others right now," Honore said finally. "I'll come, and I'll contact them. But I don't know how long—"

Oliver suddenly grabbed my shoulders and pushed me down behind the little grey hatchback we'd been standing beside. He hit the pavement beside me with a grunt and I felt the prickle of magic pass over our heads. The hair on the back of my neck stood up. I smelled the ozone scent of a nearby lightning strike, although nothing seemed to blow up. It was followed by an oily, dark redolence that nearly made me cough. The smell of the demon's magic.

"What the hell?" I started, but Oliver cut me off.

"I glanced over and saw him lift his arm toward us like he was going to do something. I just knew it couldn't be good," he gasped. "Shit! Are they coming?"

I'd dropped my phone, and I scrabbled for it on the pavement. The screen flicked to life, but the call was gone. "She's coming," I told Oliver. "Honore's coming. We just have to—"

"Hold out till she gets here?" Oliver finished. "Geez, that sounds like something out of a bad western."

"Shh." I strained to listen for footsteps, gauge where the demon was now. I got to a squat and raised my phone to the car's side window, pressing the buttons to take a quick picture. I studied the image on the screen. Although it was blurry, taken through the windows on either side of the car, I could make out the hospital doors and the figure standing in front of them.

"Okay, he's not coming after us," I said. "That's good."

"Maybe he's trying to warn us off," Oliver said. "Doesn't want to draw too much attention to himself. How does he know we recognize him?"

"No idea. Maybe he doesn't. Let's move a bit, just in case." Keeping low, I scuttled to the front end of the grey car and eased around the back of a truck next to it, calculating that the demon didn't have line of sight from the hospital doors. Oliver followed me. I crossed the short distance to the next row of cars and moved another row back next to a dark blue sedan, still confident we were out of sight.

I felt another frisson of *something* in the air, although it wasn't as close this time. I ducked and hunched my shoulders involuntarily. Oliver swore.

Two rows away, the grey car exploded.

CHAPTER FOUR

I don't carry weapons. That might seem odd, in my line of work, but honestly, violence just doesn't happen to or around me personally all that often. I usually come into a case *after* the violence, if any is involved, has already happened. Truthfully, I like it that way. Weapons usually only serve to complicate matters.

But when the car exploded, I felt like I wouldn't have minded that little complication.

I didn't scream, although Oliver let out a yelp that turned into a whimper he quickly stifled. We both threw our arms over our heads against the rain of shrapnel peppering the cars and pavement around us.

"Hey!" A man's voice sounded from the other side of the parking lot, and I heard advancing footsteps. I chanced a look over the hood of the car and saw a tall, sandy-haired man in a brown leather jacket making his way through the parking lot toward the hospital. I almost called out to him to be careful, but I realized he was taking care to stay behind the cover of the cars as he moved. He pulled down the zipper of his coat and yanked a handgun from a chest holster.

I didn't think he'd seen me, with his eyes glued to the front of the hospital. I peered through the windows and saw the demon still standing there. This was the first chance I'd had to really study him. His black hair slicked back from a widow's peak above that pale, black-traced skin. His face was narrow, the chin almost pointed. His legs and arms seemed just slightly too long—something you might overlook unless you were really looking for it. No-one else had left the hospital, which was weird, since it was a busy place. Although I suppose an explosion in the parking lot might encourage folks to stay inside.

As I watched, the demon raised a hand toward the man.

"Watch out!" I yelled as soon as I saw the motion. "Get down!"

Although the sudden sound of my voice might have startled him, the guy hit the ground without delay. Nothing exploded, but the ozone smell came again, stronger this time. I realized with a sinking feeling that I'd probably just given our new position away to the demon.

"You all right?" the newcomer called, and I

assumed he was talking to me.

"So far, so good," I answered. "Just get down if he moves."

The wail of distant sirens reached us then, and closer, I heard the crunch of tires as a car pulled into the driveway. I risked another look and saw an older-model green hatchback edge cautiously into the lot. I could just make out Honore's face behind the wheel, and she'd brought one of the other witches with her. I sagged against the side of the sedan. "Cavalry's here," I told Oliver.

"I'm not relaxing just yet," he said. "Who's our other friend?"

"No idea, but he's got a gun," I said. "I'm assuming undercover cop. Or just off-duty, maybe."

Oliver frowned. "That's not great. Cops like explanations for things."

He had a point, but I didn't see much sense in worrying about that yet.

"Police," the tall man called to the demon, confirming my suspicion. "Stay where you are."

I half-stood so I could see what was happening. The cop had his gun trained on the hospital doors, which I'm sure wasn't the most comfortable position to be in. The demon stared at him, apparently unfazed, but his head whipped toward the witches when Honore opened her door. I saw Jo emerge from the passenger side. She held a short canister in one hand and a tablet in the other. A crystal on a cord around her neck reflected prismatic colours in the watery autumn sunlight.

"Ladies, please return to your vehicle," the cop called. "We have a potentially dangerous situation here."

Honore and Jo ignored him. Honore raised her own tablet and began to intone something that buzzed in my ears like a nearby bee, but I couldn't make out words. Flickers of magic aura danced in the cold air around her.

The demon hissed, and I glanced back to him to see him bare sharp, white teeth before he turned and sprinted away in the direction he'd come from.

"Hey! Stop!" the cop yelled, and he started after the demon, even though I was sure he could see just as well as I could that it would be futile. The demon moved with—well, *inhuman* speed, and the cop would have to weave through multiple rows of cars before he could even really start running. I could have told him that, but odds were he wasn't going to listen to me. He dashed past us without a glance in our direction.

I stood up straight and Honore and Jo headed for me. "Acacia, are you all right?" Honore asked.

Oliver got to his feet then, brushing futilely at the mud and friction burns on his previously immaculate clothes. The grey flight jacket seemed to have escaped damage, but the knees of his khakis were a ruin.

"We're fine," I said before he could start to complain. "We think he must have intended to get in and see Chloe."

"Is that what you were doing here?" Jo asked in an icy voice. Belatedly I remembered they'd asked us to leave Chloe alone for now. Well, it was too late to do anything but brazen it out.

"Yes. We needed more information, so we stopped in to see how she was doing. We had no intention of bothering her if she wasn't up to it," I added defiantly.

"And was she? Up to it?" Honore asked. Her tone wasn't quite as chilly as Jo's, but it wasn't what you'd call warm, either.

"She seemed agitated," I said truthfully. "And she might have tried to cast a spell at us."

Jo's eyes widened. "She was conscious?"

"Not exactly." I was in the middle of explaining what had happened when the tall cop returned. He was speaking on a cell phone and he really didn't look happy. The distant sirens continued to grow closer, their wails fading in and out oddly through the surrounding buildings.

Jo slid the canister into her pocket. It looked to me like pepper spray, although unfamiliar sigils glowed faintly blue along the sides of the metal.

The cop ended his call and said to the four of us in general, "Would someone like to tell me what happened here?"

What was left of the grey car burned merrily, sending black smoke blooming above the parking lot, and the sirens had drawn a lot closer. I really, really wanted us all out of there before things got more awkward.

"I don't know," I said, putting as much frightened innocence into my voice as I could. "My cousin and I were just leaving the hospital when that guy started acting crazy. I think he must have shot the engine of that car or something. We were just trying to stay out of his way. Maybe someone inside saw something more."

The cop had nice grey eyes, but they regarded me with more than a little skepticism.

"Do I know you?" he asked. He looked from me to Oliver as if rifling through some internal memory storage.

"I don't think so," I said cautiously.

He turned to Honore and Jo. "You ladies all right?" He must have been too focused on the demon to have noticed the part the witches had played in the creature's sudden withdrawal.

Honore nodded and put on an innocent face. I noticed her French-Canadian accent became more pronounced. "Officer, this is frightening. What happened to that car?"

The fire truck pulled into the parking lot just then, killed the siren, and wove its way toward the burning car. "Do you need us to make a statement or something?" I asked. "Not that we saw much, but we could do that."

The cop looked at the approaching fire truck. I knew he'd have to go talk to the firefighters, too. "Give me your names, please," he said, calling up a notebook app on his phone. "Go into the station later today, or tomorrow at the latest, and just give your statements there, all right?" He took down names for all four of us, and phone numbers, too. I gave him the office number, and Oliver looked daggers at me because that left him having to give his cell number or raise uncomfortable questions about why we shared a number.

People opened the door of the hospital now and peered out, cautious and curious. I knew the officer was seeing multiple things he should be doing to control the crowd until another squad car arrived. The urgent wail of another siren drew steadily closer, so I knew that wouldn't be long. "Thanks, officer, we will. What's your name, by the way?"

I don't know what I asked him that; I didn't really need it. It just came out. Might have been those grey eyes. I thought they'd be nice if they weren't looking at me with such an unnerving level of suspicion.

"Detective Ames," he said. "Ellis Ames. Please don't forget to go in."

"We won't," I promised, and I thought I heard Oliver stifle a snort beside me. With a final unsatisfied glance over us, Detective Ames headed for the firefighters and the crowd outside the hospital door.

"Will you stop by the shop later?" Honore asked. "We should talk about this with the others."

I'd been thinking the same thing, so we set a time and the witches climbed back into their car, reversing out of the lot past an incoming squad car.

"We won't," Oliver mimicked in a ridiculous falsetto that sounded nothing like my voice.

"Oh, stop it," I said. "I was trying to throw him off the scent. The last thing we need are normal cops poking around in this and cluelessly taking on a demon. That was super bad timing, him showing up when he did."

"Tell me about it," Oliver said, "although he did provide a distraction. The demon had to split his attention between us and the good detective."

I said nothing as we finally hurried to the car and climbed inside out of the wind. I was wondering why the detective hadn't asked how, if we hadn't seen anything, I'd known to warn him when the demon threw—whatever it was, at him. Further up the parking lot, the firefighters had the car fire mostly under control, and police officers worked to keep back a growing crowd.

"So, what's next?" Oliver asked, after he'd buckled his seatbelt and sat waiting for me to start the car. "Back to the Internet to research best practices for confronting malevolent demons? I feel like that was a gap in our research earlier."

I stared at his fingers, nervously and repeatedly tracing the contours of the dog amulet. "What about your friend? Could she—or he—help us? I'd love to talk with someone who knows about the Practice before we meet with our clients again. Instead of relying on what we can dig up online."

"What friend?" Then he realized I was staring at the amulet and began to shake his head. His fingers closed over the talisman, hiding it from sight. "Oh, no. We're not involving him in this any more than he already is."

"I just want to talk to him. If he sells all this magical

stuff," I waved my thumb with the wide protection ring on it in front of Oliver's eyes, "he can probably help us more than a dozen Practice chat rooms."

"No."

"Look, he doesn't have to get involved in the case. This will just be him talking to us, answering a few questions. Helping us figure out what's going on and what to do next."

Oliver glared at me. "Acacia, is there any part of my life that can stay private while I'm working for you?"

I turned the key in the ignition and reached over to pat his arm. "Of course there is. And I'll let you know as soon as I figure out what it is."

Oliver punished me for my insolence by refusing to tell me anything about where we were going or the witch we were going to meet until we reached our destination. We drove across town from the hospital and Oliver directed me to a street only a few blocks from the Olympia Investigations office. The area was mostly residential, but one of the houses had the intentionally uneven rooflines and mismatched windows of storybook architecture. It also sported a brightly-painted sign mounted on the neat white fence bordering the road. Oliver pointed, and we pulled up in front of it and got out.

"*The Patient Frog*?" I read from the sign. In smaller letters underneath, it advertised *Metaphysical Provender*. I raised my eyebrows at Oliver.

"Don't be weird," he told me. "Remember who we are."

Well, he was right. Nothing should really surprise me any more.

The barren stems of tall hollyhocks bowed along the path to the front door. A couple of months ago they would have been buzzing with bees, but now the seed pods rattled in the wind and only a few withered, curling leaves dotted the stalks. A second sign, on the door, proclaimed *Ring and Walk In*. Oliver pressed the button and a few muffled bars from the overture of *Wicked* sounded from inside. Oliver pushed open the door without waiting, and I followed him inside. We stood in what was probably a former living room but had been converted into shop space. Shelves lined the walls, overflowing with incense, oils, crystals, candles, polished stones, jewelry, plants, dried herbs, and assorted other occult paraphernalia. The bits of wall visible between shelves displayed multiple bright paint colours. A collection of small, mismatched tables scattered the room as well, as if frozen in place in the middle of a game of tag. Navigating this space in the dark would be nigh impossible. The room was as heavily scented as the coven's beauty shop had been, but it seemed both lighter and earthier. More essential, somehow.

And to my surprise, the space held a heavy infusion of magical energy just like the coven's wardroom, as if magic use was a common occurrence within these walls. Was Oliver's friend an actual *witch*? Or did he merely entertain a lot of Practitioner customers, who tried out charms, potions, and spells in the shop? I shot a sharp glance at Oliver, but he was studiously not looking at me.

A beaded curtain at the back of the room swished aside, and a man ducked through. He wasn't overly tall, about my height, with skin that might have been dark by way of genetics or a lifetime spent outdoors. His head was completely bald, and with his slightly protruding eyes, he did remind me a bit of a frog. I wondered distractedly if that's where the shop got its name. He was dressed in faded jeans and a tunic-style shirt striped in a marvelous assortment of bright colours.

"Oliver!" he called in a booming, friendly voice. "You're back! And you've finally brought Acacia to meet me, unless I'm sadly mistaken."

He deftly wove through the obstacle course of tables and shook Oliver's hand, then took one of mine in both of his. For his stature, his hands were huge, and mine was enveloped. His dark brown eyes were warm with evident delight as he said, "I'm so pleased to meet you, my dear. Oliver holds you in the highest regard. I'm Robin."

"Acacia Sheridan," I responded automatically, then realized how ridiculous that was since he obviously knew who I was already. "It's nice to meet you, too. What a wonderful shop!" I knew that also sounded lame as soon as the words left my lips, but I was inwardly berating Oliver for not preparing me at all. Highest regard, my ass. I glanced at him and he offered me a smug smile. He was enjoying this.

But Robin sent a loving glance around the room. "It is, isn't it? I enjoy what I do so much. Helping other people really is the most rewarding thing in life. But in your line of work, you understand that, too." He released my hand with another smile and turned to Oliver. "So, everything all right? You walked into the lion's den and emerged unscathed?"

There was a gentle note of teasing in his voice, but it was also a serious question. This man wasn't making fun of Oliver's fears. Then his gaze travelled down to Oliver's scuffed and muddied pants and my dirt-streaked jeans and his expression changed, turning grave.

Before he could ask anything else, Oliver shrugged. "It was fine. But we have some questions that Acacia thought you might be able to help with."

Okay, he was putting the responsibility for us being here squarely on me. That was fine. "I don't know how much Oliver has told you—"

But a frown had puckered Robin's forehead and he put a hand up to hover next to my cheek. "And what's happened here?"

I touched my face automatically, realizing the marks of Chloe's fingers must not have faded completely yet—or perhaps a bruise was rising to mark the spot. "Oh, it's nothing. The witch who was hurt in the summoning—we tried to talk to her but she got a little freaked out. I don't think she even realized who I was—"

"Wait here," Robin commanded, and crossed to a shelf on the right-hand wall. He ran a finger along a row of small ointment pots, then selected one and brought it over to us, unscrewing the lid. He presented it to me. "You won't need much. Just lightly massage it in."

I swiped a bit of the pale pink cream onto my index finger and smoothed it over my cheek. It tingled on contact, then felt cool and soothing as I rubbed it into the mistreated skin. I realized with a start that the spot had been tender, aching slightly, although I'd been ignoring it with everything else that had happened. Now all the residual discomfort faded. I smiled. "Thank you! That feels wonderful!"

Robin tucked the small jar into my hand and closed my fingers around it. "The perfect remedy for small indignities, especially if there's malice behind them," he told me. "And don't even think about paying for it. A gift is a sacred thing."

I blinked and tucked the jar into my pocket. "All right, then thank you again. So this case we're on—"

"Tea!" Robin declared. "Tea absolutely must be the next order of business. Follow me through to the kitchen; it's a much more soothing atmosphere for the telling of distressing tales. We'll sit and have tea while you relate your experiences."

The man turned and vanished through the beaded curtain again. Oddly, I wasn't upset. If Oliver did that when I was trying to explain something to him, I'd be annoyed.

"Let's go," Oliver said. "Tea is a serious matter in this house." He followed Robin and I trailed after them. I admit I had a burning curiosity to see more of the place.

Beyond the curtained doorway, the house lost its occult trappings but none of its charm. We followed a wood-floored hallway past a cozy living room, where iron-railed stairs wound up one wall to the partial upper floor and presumably at least one bedroom. The downstairs hallway emerged into a yellow-walled kitchen with blue and white gingham curtains at the windows and an ancient-looking mahogany table at one end. Four mismatched but oddly complementary wooden chairs waited around it. At the other end of the room an actual cooking hearth sat inside a fieldstone surround. Space had been found for modern appliances, too, and Robin set a red enamel kettle on the stove as I walked in.

"Sit," he ordered genially, and Oliver complied, pulling out a chair at the table. I did the same. Hanging wire baskets held potatoes, onions, and other vegetables, and bunches of drying herbs tucked up near the beams of the vaulted ceiling. This was a kitchen in which someone actually *cooked*, and I thought of my well-used ancient microwave with a pang of guilt.

"All right," Robin said, spilling golden-brown muffins from a jar on the counter onto a floral-patterned plate and setting it on the table. "Your clients have a demon problem."

I flashed a look at Oliver as Robin bustled around the kitchen, pulling butter from the fridge, small plates from a cupboard and knives from a drawer. Oliver shrugged.

"That's right," I said as Robin laid everything on the table. "I don't know *how much* Oliver has told you—"

"Just the bare facts," Robin assured me. "So I would know what protections he might need. He didn't share anything confidential, I'm sure."

The scents of chocolate and banana crept into my perception, and when I reached for a muffin, it felt warm. But Robin hadn't heated them...had he? I glanced up sharply, and sure enough, a weak yellow aura of just-used magic limned his fingertips. I'd figured him simply for a supplier of magical items, but now I knew his involvement went much further than that—he was an actual Practitioner. The idea that Oliver could have a friend who was a witch had never occurred to me, given his past experience and his obvious discomfort with Honore and the other coven witches. Oliver had said nothing about Robin's calling—probably so he wouldn't have to explain it to me. What a rat. But I'd have to deal with that later. I blinked and focused on what Robin was saying.

"I understand you don't have much to go on. If we knew the type of spirit that had been summoned, it would be a big help. Can you pinpoint where he's been appearing?"

"I didn't think to ask my clients that. They said they'd been able to locate him a few times through scrying but could never get to the location fast enough to catch him with a geas. We were trying to arm ourselves with more information before we actually go out looking, but then we encountered him ourselves today—at the hospital."

Robin raised his eyebrows. "Which explains your slightly rumpled state, I assume?"

Oliver nodded.

"All right. Any idea what he was doing there?"

"We think he was trying to get to the witch who served as the keystone in the summoning. She's still in that hospital."

Robin nodded thoughtfully. "You're probably right. But if they can tell you something about the other areas where he's been noted, there could be a clue there. And also a starting point for you two to start looking for him."

I felt stupid for not asking that seemingly obvious question. "We're meeting them tonight, so I'll ask. We're suspicious that one of the witches—the keystone—might have had dealings with this demon before," I said. "The others in the coven hadn't said so, but maybe they didn't know. We read online that a previous entanglement—I'm sure I'm not using the correct terminology—might explain why this spirit appeared and not the one they wanted, and why it attacked her."

The kettle whistled, and Robin got up to see to it, pouring the boiling water into a teapot painted with delicate roses. "That might explain it," he said, wrapping the teapot in a bright flannel cozy and bringing it to the table to pour. "That kind of connection can be hard to break if enough time hasn't passed. And a lot depends on the strength of the demon, the experience and will of the Practitioner...without more details all I can do is speculate."

"We'd appreciate any help at all," I said.

Robin wrapped his hands around his mug, contemplating the steam rising from the tea inside. "Let's make a fairly safe assumption: if the coven knew of the keystone's previous, recent connection to a demon—a demon they did *not* want to summon—they would have taken better precautions, or ensured that someone else acted as keystone. They would have known of the danger."

"So you think they didn't know," I said.

He nodded. "Unless they are lying to you about everything—in which case, why hire you at all?"

"Good question," I said, "and I don't have an

answer for it."

"All right, let's assume they aren't lying to you about everything—although they may be lying to you about *something*, or holding information back. Witches are notorious for liking to play things close to the chest," he said with a smile. "But I don't think they'd take the chance of letting her stand keystone if they knew she had a previous connection."

"Why wouldn't she tell them, though?" I asked. "Or at least come up with some reason to avoid being keystone? She must have known it was dangerous."

Robin nodded gravely. "She must. Or at least suspected it could be an issue. Thus, the question must be, what did she hope to accomplish?"

I pulled a deep sigh. "The other witches may have an answer—if they'll tell me."

"It's the logical place to start. I assume the keystone herself is unavailable for questioning."

"Not for lack of trying," I said, "but for now, no, there's no help there."

"And not much here, I'm afraid," Robin said with a sigh. "Although I'm willing to help all I can. I just need more information."

"We'll see what we can get," I said. "We'll probably be back."

Oliver groaned, but I ignored him. Robin was too

good a resource to waste. "One more thing before we go," I said. "Do you have any demon wards in stock?"

Robin smiled, and Oliver sighed and rolled his eyes. "Let's go back to the shop," Robin said, "I think I know just the thing...

CHAPTER FIVE

Like good, responsible citizens, Oliver and I reported in to the police station and gave our statements about what had happened in the hospital parking lot. Yes, we kept it vague and played "dumb." We probably wouldn't have gotten away with it if either Detective Ellis Ames or my sort-of-friends, Detectives Sasha Crombie and Dmitri Crux, had been present for the interviews. Crombie and Crux pretended not to know about the peculiarities of my PI business, but in truth they were simply happy to turn a blind eye to anything that seemed a little too unusual and trust me to take care of it. I wasn't sure if that was complimentary or just self-serving. As soon as something happened that was serious enough, though, they knew and I knew that they'd have to take the blinders off. They'd be hard pressed to believe I didn't know more than I was telling when a car suddenly detonated in a parking lot where Oliver and I were standing. Detective Ames had been on the spot, and I felt reasonably certain he hadn't bought my wide-eyed innocent schtick, either. He just couldn't do much about it at the time.

Anyway, we gave our didn't-see-much-and-understood-even-less tales and left the station with only about half an hour lost. It was late afternoon now, and I had to admit the day was wearing me thin.

"I sure would like to take the rest of the day off," I told Oliver as we stood by my car in the station parking lot. The chill wind had calmed but the day remained cool, and I kept my hands in my pockets. The trees studding the edge of the police station lot still held onto most of their autumn colours, but a few red leaves crinkled under my feet. "But I promised to go and talk to the witches again. And now we have to ask them some tough questions about Chloe."

Oliver nodded and rolled his neck. "I wonder if we could do it after dinner? I need a hot shower and a change of clothes, and something to eat before I feel normal again."

"For some values of normal," I said with a half-hearted grin.

"Not even going to argue with you at this point," he said in a tired voice. "Do you think the witches will do anything about Chloe being alone in the hospital? And that guy maybe trying to get to her?"

I shrugged. "I assume they will. I thought I'd get to bring it up this afternoon. But I don't expect they need me to tell them she might be in danger after this afternoon."

Leaning against the side of my ancient Honda, I sent Honore a quick text asking if we could meet around 6:30 or 7. She agreed, and instructed that the shop would be closed but we could knock at the rear delivery door whenever we arrived.

"We have a reprieve," I told Oliver. "Actually, if you want to skip this one, you can. I think you've put in your hours today."

"I can be ready to go again for this evening," he said. "I'd like to hear what they have to say about the demon showing up at the hospital. And whether they're ready to be more forthcoming about Chloe."

"All right, hop in," I told him. "I'll drop you at your place and swing by to get you again later. But just remember, this is the job you didn't want to work on at all, and now I can't get you to take a break from it."

He made a face at me and we talked about other things as we crossed the city. I told him I'd see him in a couple of hours when he climbed out in front of his building, but I turned out to be wrong about that.

I'd cleaned up and was eating a slice of cold pizza fortuitously left in my fridge when my phone buzzed.

The ID showed Detective Sasha Crombie's number in the call display. Surprised, I picked up. "Detective?"

"Hey, Sheridan," she said, but her voice sounded flat. "We have something I think you'd be—interested in."

I took the phone away from my ear and stared at it. The detectives were coming to *me* for input? This was new. And I wasn't sure I liked it. I listened again. "Okay, tell me what's up."

"I think you ought to see this," she said. "Okay if someone swings by and gives you a lift to a crime scene?"

"Uh, sure. I'm supposed to be somewhere in half an hour or so. Will this take long?"

"Is it at all possible for you to postpone whatever it is?" Detective Crombie asked evenly.

Well, this was sounding worse and worse. But the witches could wait until tomorrow morning. Maybe this couldn't. "I'll be here," I told her, and she said "Great" and broke the connection.

I sent quick texts to Honore and Oliver telling them something had come up and we'd have to reschedule, and they both replied. Honore said she'd gather the coven in the morning. I dumped the rest of my pizza in the trash, having lost my appetite, and glanced around the apartment, wondering if there was anything special

I should be taking. Detective Crombie hadn't been exactly bubbling over with information for me.

In the end I shrugged into my jacket, checked that the ring Oliver had given me was snug on my thumb, and hung the amulet I'd bought from Robin around my neck, slipping it inside my t-shirt out of sight. It was a silver tray pendant with a blue-green cat's-eye stone set into the tray. Robin had described the distinct white band of reflective light marking the stone's centre as *chatoyancy,* and showed me how moving the stone made it appear that the line opened and closed like a cat's eye. He assured me it was a strong ward against evil and turned it over to show me the tiny sigils elegantly engraved on the pendant's silver back. He'd pressed me to take it as a gift, but I'd insisted on paying him for it. The pendant settled cold against my skin but quickly warmed. In my line of work, I could use all the protection against evil I could get. But I didn't need it to be so obvious that people would start asking awkward questions.

Anyway, I didn't want to appear too eager since the police were asking for my help for a change, so I stood at my window overlooking the street while I waited for the pickup, mulling over the problem of how to safely catch a demon who could blow up cars from a hundred feet away.

I'd just concluded that actually catching him was going to be the witches' job anyway, when a police car pulled up outside the building. I headed downstairs to meet them, pulling on my jacket as I went. I wasn't going to make Crombie and Crux walk all the way to my door when they knew I was expecting them.

Except when I stepped outside and headed for the cruiser, I realized that neither Crombie nor Crux had come to collect me. It was Detective Ellis Ames. My stomach gave a lurch. *The game is up.* He watched me approach the car with an expressionless face.

I made myself smile normally at him as I opened the passenger door and climbed inside. "Evening, Detective."

"Miss Sheridan," he was all he said, and put the car in gear.

"Oliver and I went in and gave our statements this afternoon," I blurted. I immediately wanted to bite my tongue, because if he was here picking me up about something Crombie and Crux knew I should be involved in, it was far too late to keep up my dumb innocent bystander charade. I wanted to wait and see how he was going to handle it, though.

"I read them," he said blandly.

I looked out the car window, wondering where we were going but sensing that maybe it would be better if

I just stayed quiet.

Detective Ames wasn't going to let me do that.

"You know," he said, turning the cruiser in the direction of the most northerly of the three bridges connecting the halves of the city bisected by the river, "I thought your name sounded familiar when you gave it to me today."

"Oh?" I said cautiously.

He tossed a glance my way and then put his eyes back on the road. "Crombie and Crux have mentioned you from time to time. They seem to think you're—"

I waited, but he didn't finish the sentence, as if he were searching for just the right word. "Special?" I suggested finally.

The corner of his mouth twitched, as if it wanted to smile. "Involved in some...unusual cases."

"Well, that's true," I said. "But let me point out that Crombie and Crux have never evinced any desire to poke into my 'unusual' cases too closely, so you might not want to take everything they say as gospel."

We'd crossed the bridge now, to the east side of the city. Oliver's apartment building was over here, and for a paralyzing moment I thought maybe something bad had happened to him. Then I remembered with relief that we'd texted *after* Crombie had called me.

"They actually admitted as much to me," Ames

said. "They suggested that I might want to take the same approach."

"And what do you think of that suggestion?"

He drove in silence for a moment and then said, "On balance, I'm happier knowing things than not knowing them."

"But you can't be sure about that until you know what a particular thing is," I noted. "Then once you know it, you might think you were happier before you knew it."

This time he turned and looked fully at me. "Are you always this annoying?"

"Thanks, I like you, too," I said. "And the answer to that question depends entirely on who you ask." I knew exactly how Oliver would answer it, but I wasn't going to tell Ames that.

He got quiet again after that, but we drove for only about another minute anyway. Then up ahead I saw the telltale flashes of blue and red lights, and I knew this was not going to be good.

CHAPTER SIX

At first glance, it was a stereotypical crime scene—yellow warning tape marking a perimeter and various official vehicles parked haphazardly nearby. I saw the ME's van and wondered if my friend Caro Lewis was on the scene. I rather expected so. She was the head of the department and liked to see things for herself.

I didn't make a move to leave the cruiser when Detective Ames pulled it over and shut off the engine. I turned to him. "Okay, I don't usually find myself at actual crime scenes, so I'd like a little preparation about what I'm doing here and what I should expect to see."

He nodded. "Fair enough. It's a homicide scene—I'm sure you figured that much out already. Two bodies discovered in the alleyway behind a club called Strange and Wonderful. The place wasn't even open yet—they unlock the doors at 8. Cleaner getting the place ready for the night took some garbage out back and made the find." He took a breath. "It's not pretty."

I swallowed past a dry mouth, suddenly glad I hadn't finished the rest of my pizza. "And I'm here, because?"

Detective Ames blew out a sigh. "Because someone in the neighbourhood described seeing a guy that sounded a heck of a lot like our friend from the hospital today. And because I think there was more to that incident than you told me. Or mentioned in your statement. And because Crombie and Crux told me you'd want to help, as long as I didn't try to push you into it."

I had my own ideas about being pushed into it, considering that I felt Sasha Crombie had...maybe not lied, but certainly misled me about who was coming to pick me up. However, I could let that go for now. It seemed like Ames was being straight with me. I figured I could at least try to be straight with him.

"Fair enough. Yes, there was more to today's incident than I told you. But," I held up a finger and continued quickly when he opened his mouth, "you may or may not be happy with or even believe my explanation. That'll be up to you. I do want to help, though, if I can." I drew in a breath. "So I guess you'd better show me what happened."

He studied me for a long moment, then seemed to

decide. "Let's go."

I kept pace with him as we made our way through the lowering twilight, into the alley behind Strange and Wonderful. I'd never been inside the club myself. I had it pegged as catering to a younger crowd. But every bar and club looked pretty much the same outside the back door. A none-too-clean alley strewn with debris, graffiti-streaked walls, dumpsters piled with bagged trash and an assortment of smells, mostly unpleasant. This one, while it had all those things, was also filled with differences. I stopped and took it in. Tented white evidence cards marked some of the litter, and a body lay mostly covered with a tarp near the club's back door. I caught a glimpse of a woman's white face under a spill of auburn hair and shuddered. A woman in a pale coverall, dark hair caught back in a short ponytail, knelt next to the body doing something I couldn't quite make out. Further down the alley, the surroundings flared briefly in the repeated flashes of a police photographer's camera as he took pictures near another tarp-covered form. Beyond him, a pair of beat cops stood guard at the other end of the alleyway.

Two more techs stood near the back wall of the building, examining what looked like paint spatters. I turned away a little too quickly. I knew after the first glance that it wasn't paint.

Detective Ames' hand caught my elbow gently. "You okay?"

I took a deep gulp of air and nodded. "No. Yeah. Just took me by surprise there."

"You don't have to look at the bodies if you don't want to—there's no reason to think you could identify them. Let's have a chat with the medical examiner." He raised his voice. "Dr. Lewis? Do you have a moment?"

The dark-haired woman in the coverall stood and turned toward us, a slight frown marring her smooth features. It disappeared when she saw me, though, and she hurried over.

"Dr. Lewis, this is—"

Caro ignored Detective Ames, throwing her arms around me in a hug. The Mi'kmaw woman was one of my best friends, but it was rare for me to encounter her at an actual crime scene. Intellectually I knew this was part of her job, but I usually saw her in her office in the hospital's chilly basement if I had a question about a case. "When I saw the bodies, I thought you might have an interest in this, but I didn't think they'd drag you down here for it," she said, and pulled back. She gave Ames a look that could be described as disapproving, if we were being generous.

"Okay," Ames said. "No introductions necessary, I see. Dr. Lewis, can you give Ms. Sheridan a run-down on what we have here? And I wonder if you'd explain what you mean about thinking she'd be interested when you saw the bodies?"

Caro sent him a challenging look. "You're the ones who brought her here, you must have a reason, right?"

Ames looked like he wasn't sure what to say to that.

Caro shrugged and went on. "Two victims, one male and one female, both in their mid-to-late twenties at a guess." She glanced over her shoulder at the nearby tarp and grimaced. "They might have been chased in here, judging by some of the marks we found near the entrance to the alley. It was...messy. I might think they'd been attacked by a wild animal if—" She broke off.

"If what?"

"If we were further north, I'd suspect a *ki'kwa'ju.*"

I must have looked blank at the Mi'kmaq word, because it was one I hadn't heard before. "Wolverine," she said. "Vicious animals, stronger than their size would make you think. The victims are badly cut up. A lot of blood spray, which you can see on the wall there." Caro nodded to the area next to the door. "I think whoever did it attacked the woman first, the man tried to run at some point, and the assailant brought him down like a coyote on a deer. At first glance, the wounds look more like claw damage than something done with a blade. They're ragged."

This must have been the first Detective Ames had heard about that. "We haven't had any reports of wild animals in the area, have we?"

Caro Lewis gave him a look as if he were dense. "I didn't say they *were* attacked by a wild animal. I said that's what it looks like."

"So it was a blade after all?"

She gave him a piercing look. "Those aren't the only two options. Do you even know why you have Acacia here?"

Detective Ames' grey eyes went wide, glanced around the scene as if the answer lay in plain sight. "Okay, I'm starting to suspect that I don't. I'm clearly out of the loop here. Is there any way you two could see your way clear to bring me inside it? You'll notice I'm asking nicely."

Caro's lips twitched, suppressing a sudden smile. I knew she wasn't really annoyed with Ames, but she liked to exert control over what she considered "her" crime scenes. And she was protective of me, knowing I was out of my element here. "He's asking nicely, Acacia. There's a coffee shop just down the block; I passed it on my way. Why don't you go there, get a couple of coffees, and tell him what's going on. Then you can come back with my takeout coffee, and tell *me* what's going on."

Ames shook his head, and I didn't think he was going to go for it, but maybe Caro's reputation preceded her and he thought better of crossing her at a scene. As darkness fell, the air got even colder, and the thought of what had happened here chilled me further. I shivered. I don't know if that convinced him, but I didn't argue when Ames agreed to Caro's suggestion.

Ten minutes later, we found ourselves at a quiet table near the window of the shop, two steaming mugs on the table between us. I wasn't sure where to start, and I had to consider exactly how much I was going to tell him, so I curled my hands around my mug and waited for Ellis Ames to begin the conversation.

"I feel like we got off to a bad start," he said, after sipping carefully at his coffee. "And I suspect whatever you're going to tell me isn't going to be easy. So let's just say I'm open to starting over."

I took a pull of my own mug and pondered how to go about this. If he was willing to meet me even halfway, that was a good thing. As long as that commitment lasted past the first few revelations. But obviously Sasha Crombie thought he could handle the truth, and so did Caro, and they must know him better than I did.

"All right," I said finally. "You know I'm a private

investigator."

He nodded.

"Oliver, who was with me—he's my office assistant, and also my cousin."

"Okay."

I tapped my fingers against the side of the mug. "What's your feeling on things that are...let's just say, a little outside the normal range of experience for most people?"

Ames tilted his head and regarded me, frowning slightly. "What kinds of things?"

There was no easy way to say it. "Supernatural things. Paranormal things. Weird things."

He sat back in his chair with his lips pursed, but at least he didn't laugh. "I'm...a skeptic."

"Okay. That means this is going to be hard for you. I'm sorry." I took a sip of coffee. "Most of my clients are not normal humans. They exist right here among the rest of us, but most people don't understand their true natures, and wouldn't be able to tell them apart from normal humans anyway. Not just by looking."

He raised his eyebrows. "We're not talking about aliens here, are we? Like extraterrestrials?"

"Would that be easier for you?"

"Easier compared to what?"

I sighed. "My last three clients before this case

were, in order, a ghost, a mythological goddess, and a vampire who lives a few blocks from here."

He studied his coffee cup, brows knit. He looked out the window for a minute, although all he'd be able to see against the early evening darkness was our reflections in the cozily-lit shop. Then he returned his gaze to me. "Honestly, aliens might have been easier."

I smiled. "Well, I haven't had one of them yet, but I'm not prepared to guarantee they don't exist. What I can tell you is that my current client—well, clients—are a coven of practicing urban witches, and their problem is that they've accidentally summoned a malevolent spirit. What some people might call a demon."

There was another pause while he digested this.

"I know this is a lot to take in." I had to admit, he appeared to be taking his promise to keep an open mind seriously.

He shook his head. "No, it's all right. I'm just rearranging my mental furniture. So that was a demon in the parking lot today?"

I nodded. "He caught us by surprise when he showed up."

"And I'm guessing the theory is that he's also responsible for the deaths of those two people. That's why Crombie and Crux put me onto you."

I shrugged. "We'll have to get more information

from Caro Lewis, and I'll have to do some more research before I could even attempt to give you an opinion on that. Honestly, this is my first demon. And yeah, Crombie and Crux don't come right out and admit it, but they at least suspect there's something weird about most of my cases."

He tried a half smile. "But after vampires, surely a demon is a piece of cake?"

"To tell you the truth, the vampire was a pretty decent person, and we've become friends," I told him. "Vampires get a bad rap with the whole blood-drinking thing, but there's a lot more to them than that."

I had a sudden memory of Valia Northern attacking the thugs who'd been killing people from a local homeless shelter and shuddered despite the warmth of the coffee shop and the steaming mug in my hands. The blood-drinking thing wasn't something you could discount entirely, no matter how nice the vampire in question might be.

But we weren't here to talk about Valia. "I think the demon was at the hospital today looking for one of the witches who was responsible for summoning him. She's still a patient there following the summoning that went wrong. From what my investigation has turned up so far, she may or may not be somehow working with him, unknown to her coven sisters. When we chased him away, maybe he was just pissed off and took it out on those folks in the alley; maybe there's more to it and there'll be a connection when we know who they are. Like I said, I don't know much about demons yet. But I did hear stories from my grandmother, who *did* know a lot about demons, and let's say it wouldn't surprise me if a random rage-killing turned out to be the explanation."

Ames looked very solemn and nodded slowly. "Let's say for the sake of argument I believe you. I mean, you seem reasonably sane and in control of your faculties."

"Gee, thanks, glad I don't look like I've broken with reality today."

"I meant it as a compliment," he said with a half-smile. "But if what you say is true, we have to get this guy, and we have to get him fast. I still don't know how he did everything he did, but between blowing up cars without a bomb and ripping people apart, he's proved he's extremely dangerous."

"Agreed. That's my job for the witches—help them track him down. Oliver and I have a...talent for finding and recognizing these types of beings, so we're a logical choice. If we find him, the witches can put a geas on him—control him," I explained when Ames looked blank. "They'll send him back where he came from, but it's a complicated process, especially with one of them still in hospital. But the geas should contain the threat until they can do that."

"I don't suppose a good old-fashioned jail cell is going to be up to the task," he said, as if he'd already figured out the answer.

I shook my head. "You were in the parking lot for part of what happened today. I don't know the extent of his powers, but I don't think brick and mortar are any match for what he's packing."

I almost saw the lightbulb go on above his head. "And those two women who showed up in the car at the hospital—"

I nodded. "They were two of my clients. They were doubtful they could do much against him without the others, but they showed up willing to try."

It was Ames' turn to drum his fingers on the scarred tabletop. "And you want me to keep this quiet, right?"

I shrugged again. "Go ahead and tell if you think anyone will believe you, but I don't think that's likely. And if you want my opinion, sending beat cops after this guy is only going to get you dead cops."

"After what I saw in the alley, I'm inclined to agree with you," he said. He fetched a deep sigh. "So we're demon-hunting. Okay, that's a new one, but let's do it."

"We? Are you sure you're—"

His mouth pressed into a thin line. "I saw those bodies. I want to help get this guy. Thing. Whatever he is. Now, how does Dr. Lewis like her coffee?"

"Black, one sugar, and a vanilla shot if they have it," I said. Detective Ames went to the counter to order it and I looked after him, considering. He'd taken all that surprisingly well. It might be nice to have a cop who'd actually work with us on this one.

On the other hand, it might just be a big pain in the ass. I rather expected Oliver to think so.

When he came back with Caro's coffee, we headed out into the now-black night.

The scene of crime team was winding down as Detective Ames and I returned to the back alley of Strange and Wonderful. Caro had packed up her bag and stood watching two techs maneuver the bodies into the back of a morgue van. She took the coffee gratefully and sipped it. She eyed Detective Ames, but spoke to me.

"Well, he's still upright, and still here," she said with a half-smile.

I nodded. "He took it pretty well, honestly."

"I'm standing right here," Ames protested.

"And don't think we don't appreciate it," Caro said.

"So, what's the bad news? What's involved here?"

I sighed. "I think it's probably a demon."

Caro pursed her lips. "That's a new one," she said finally, without the hint of a smile.

"Unfortunately, I don't know as much as I'd like to about what that means," I said. "But my main job is to find him. That's what my clients hired me to do."

"It could explain the wounds," she said contemplatively. "Large, curved claws would do this kind of damage."

Detective Ames frowned. "I'm trying to stay on board here, but the guy I saw in the hospital parking lot didn't have any kind of claws. He just had hands."

Caro shrugged. "Demons and spirits aren't confined to one shape, Detective. A wolverine spirit, like *Luks,* could assume aspects or attributes of the animal if it wanted. It lines up with my impression of those wounds."

I really had to go and talk to Robin again, ask him if he'd give me a crash course on demonology. Even Caro knew more about these things than I did.

"I'll keep my report as generic as I can," Caro told us. "Drop by tomorrow afternoon and I'll tell you anything else I find. Now I'm going home to finish my dinner."

"Thanks, Caro," I told her. "I'll let you know if

anything else happens."

"I hope you rein this one in quick," she said, and squeezed my arm. "And watch yourself, Acacia. This one's nasty."

As she walked away, I instinctively put a hand up and touched the protection pendant around my neck. The silver had warmed in proximity to my skin, so I was hardly aware of it anymore. Through my shirt the smooth roundness of the cat's-eye gem felt small and insignificant. Could it really help if I came up against rending claws and the fierce rage of a demon?

Beside me, Detective Ames had stuck his hands in his pockets, also watching Caro Lewis walk to her car. "And to think I was worried this might be a serial killer," he said laconically.

I shuddered. "Let's hope not."

"I guess I'd better get you home," he said. "Not much more to see here, I guess."

I came out of my reverie. "Let me have a look around," I said. "Now that the bodies are gone, I might be able to pick up on something."

Ames shrugged. "Whatever you think."

I made myself turn and face into the alley again. The two cops at the far end were shadowy outlines now, and only two crime scene techs remained, making final notes. I walked toward the guards, letting my gaze sweep left and right along the alleyway. If the demon had really been here, if he had used a shifter ability to take on the aspect of the animal, there might be a trace left that I could identify. Nothing so obvious as the riot of scent and colour in the witches' wardroom, a place where magical residue permeated the space. But I might catch a whiff—

I stopped. I stood near the place where the woman's body had lain. I hadn't ventured this far into the alley when we'd first arrived. But there was something here...just a hint of a dark, oily scent I recognized. I knelt and put a hand on the cracked pavement, being careful to avoid the dark splotches of drying blood. If I squinted, a faint reddish tracery of magic signature glowed on the ground, possibly in places where the demon's feet had touched down.

"He was here," I said in a low voice, and then repeated it when Ames didn't seem to hear me. "He was here."

The detective knelt beside me, following my gaze. He shook his head. "I don't see anything. How do you know?"

"It's nothing that would stand up in a courtroom," I said. "But it's what Oliver and I do. We can see people for what they are—a ghost, a vampire, a demon, whatever. We can sense the use of magic and magic abilities." I shrugged. "Stuff like that."

He snorted a soft laugh. "Yeah, stuff like that. Stuff I would have laughed at before this afternoon."

I looked over at him. He was staring at the ground as if thinking if he looked long enough, he'd be able to see the magic, too. "You saw something, or felt something, at the hospital today, didn't you? Even if your mind wouldn't let you process it right then in the middle of everything happening."

He bobbed his head, not looking at me. "I waited while the Fire Marshall investigated the burning car. I talked to the fire fighters. No-one could figure out how the fire started. It didn't make any sense. Finally, they said it was electrical, but we all knew no-one was satisfied with that." He pulled his shoulders up toward his ears and let them fall back again, as if trying to ease tension in his back. "But it was really the way you warned me to get down. I thought the guy had a gun or something I hadn't seen, but I...I *felt* it go over me, you know? Whatever he threw at me—energy or evil or magic or whatever we're going to call it—I *felt* it." He shuddered. "I'd never felt anything like that before. And I sure as hell didn't like it."

"Haha, I see what you did there," I said. "Sure as hell? Demon?"

He looked at me with one eyebrow raised.

"Sorry, just trying to lighten the mood," I said with a sigh. "Yeah, I get it. Weird feelings I get from different kinds of creatures don't freak me out personally anymore—well, unless they're the kind that are trying to kill me—but I understand that they'd make an impression. You were lucky. Most people probably wouldn't have time to think about it afterward, because they'd be dead. Welcome to your first taste of magic."

"Well, I'm not-dead because of you," he said lightly. "So thanks."

"You're very welcome."

I stood and continued down the alley, sensing the same energies when I reached the place where the demon had taken the man down. "It's either the same demon or one with the exact same signatures, and I don't even know if that's possible. I'll try to find out tomorrow."

"Please don't tell me there's a chance there are two of these things in the city."

"Highly doubtful," I said, and smile reassuringly at him. "And now, I think I'm ready to go home."

We climbed into the car and I felt weariness hit me like a wave. Ever since I'd received the call from Crombie, I'd been on high alert without even realizing it. We didn't say much on the drive back to my apartment building, mostly because I was fighting to stay awake. We were almost at my apartment when Detective Ames asked, "So, what's our next move?"

That jolted me awake. *Our?* Oh, right. The detective wanted in on the investigation. "Well, I'm meeting with the witches in the morning. I'm not sure if it would be a good idea for you to come along on that or not," I said, giving him a rueful smile. "They're my clients, and it's a pretty unusual situation for me to be sharing even that much information with the police. Once I tell them about the murders, I'll explain that there'll have to be some police involvement, but I need a chance to break this to them first."

He nodded. "Understood. But you have my number. Will you let me know what you're going to do after you talk to them? I don't want you—I just want to be in the loop, all right?"

I wondered what he'd been about to say, but I was too tired to push it. I nodded. "Sure. I'll call you when I know something more."

He glanced at my building. "You okay now? Want me to walk you in?"

I shook my head. "I think I'm fine. I know you're not going to drive away until I'm inside."

He chuckled. "You got me. Thanks, Ms. Sheridan. And thanks for being straight with me about—everything."

"Thanks for not calling me crazy," I returned lightly, "and you might as well make it Acacia. I'm not much for formalities."

"Great. I'm Ellis, then."

"Goodnight, Ellis." I got out and walked to my building, glancing around as I always did, but not feeling particularly concerned. I didn't expect the demon to come after me here; after all, how would he figure out where I lived from the brief encounter we'd had?

I still turned on all the lights in my apartment and searched it from top to bottom after Detective Ellis Ames had driven off in his car. You can't be too careful where demons are concerned.

CHAPTER SEVEN

Oliver and I arrived at Seven Sisters Health and Beauty at the appointed time the next morning. Jo let us in and turned the "Open" sign on the door to "Back Soon," and led us back to the wardroom. The six unhospitalized coven sisters were present: Honore, Jo, Blanche, Sasha, Gennai, and Trina. Blanche had been the one stirring the big pot and wearing the Hello Kitty bandanna yesterday; Trina had the blonde highlights and multiple piercings. The general mood of the group was grave. More than one of them showed the red-rimmed eyes of someone who'd been crying. They must have heard about the murders.

"I take it you've heard the news," I said, once they'd brought a couple more chairs to the boardroom table so we could all sit around it.

"I don't understand how this could happen," Honore said in a voice that threatened to break if she didn't keep tight control of it.

"He must have been angry about what happened at the hospital," I ventured.

The witches looked puzzled. "Who?" Jo asked.

"Um, the demon?"

"You think he took her?" Blanche breathed. "I was afraid of that."

I held up my hands. "Whoa, whoa. What are you all talking about? I'm talking about the murders last night."

"Murders?" Gasps ran around the room and the women looked startled. "Who was murdered?"

"Not Chloe?" Honore rasped.

I shook my head. "No, not Chloe. A man and a woman behind a club on the east side of the river. I don't know their names, but the woman had red hair. Why would you think it was Chloe?"

"Because she's gone!" Jo blurted. "She disappeared from the hospital sometime during the night. That's why we're upset!"

"She wasn't in any shape to walk out of there on her own," Oliver said. "Not when we saw her yesterday."

"I know," Honore said. "The nurses can't understand it. Gennai went around this morning with a healing philtre, and Chloe's room was empty. Everyone on the floor swears she was there whenever they checked through the night, and no-one saw her leave."

I chewed my lip for a moment and said, "Well, this complicates matters." I glanced at Oliver and he shrugged. I still had to ask what I came here to ask. "However, I still have to ask you some things about Chloe."

The witches glanced at each other. "What things?" Trina asked.

I took out my notepad. "Do you think there's a chance Chloe might have summoned this particular demon at some time in the past? Specifically, the recent past?"

Jo looked confused. "Without us knowing? I don't think so. And why would she do that?"

"I don't know," I admitted. "But Oliver and I did some research." I told them what we'd found about the binding entanglement between a summoner and a spirit. "It seemed to us that could explain why this particular demon appeared when you didn't expect him."

Honore and Jo shared a quick look I don't think they wanted me to see, but I was trying to watch all their reactions closely.

"What?"

Honore made eye contact with each of the other witches before she answered me, as if asking a silent question. She must have received an answer, because she said slowly, "We did have a little...trouble, with Chloe a few months ago."

I perked up, interested, and Oliver did, too. "What kind of trouble?"

She was obviously reluctant to explain, but she did. "We got it sorted out. She saw that what she was suggesting was wrong. It was just...Chloe wanted to try some things that not all of us were...comfortable with."

"Dark Practice?" Oliver asked in a harsh voice.

Honore shook her head. "No, not Dark. We'd never agree to that."

The other witches added their support, but then Jo said, "But if we're honest, perhaps trending that way. Methods of utilizing energy that the rest of us couldn't condone—using animals."

Oliver made a disgusted noise in the back of his throat.

Jo turned to him. "Yes. I agree. As did all the rest— that there was no place for that in our Practice."

Trina said, "Chloe backed off pretty quickly. She said she hadn't thought it through, that she was just thinking we could do more good in the community if we could increase our energy output."

I pursed my lips. "And you think she accepted your refusal to consider her suggestions?"

Honore glanced at the others. "I really thought she did," she said. "You have to know Chloe. She can be a little...impulsive. She does things without thinking them through sometimes. But she has a good heart."

"Impulsive to the point of being reckless?" I pressed. "Would she go behind your backs to follow her ideas if the rest of you didn't agree?"

No-one answered. Blanche licked her lips and said finally, "She might. Maybe she got herself into something she didn't intend."

"Can you find her?" Jo asked. "I know we haven't even found the demon yet, but maybe we should try to find Chloe first."

"The demon has started killing people," I reminded them. I knew it sounded harsh, but it was the truth. "I don't think we can let up on trying to find him. And Oliver and I will be no better than anyone else at finding Chloe. She won't stand out to us as a magical being unless she uses magic where we can see her. I think we'd better continue to concentrate on the demon. And there's something else," I told them. "Last night's murders open up a whole new problem—police involvement."

Sasha, who had been quiet this whole time, said, "The police aren't going to buy a story about a demon."

"I've found one who will," I said, "and he wants to

work with us on this. The Medical Examiner is a friend of mine, too, so we should be able to keep the supernatural element out of it—but only if we get to the demon and shut him down soon. Now, I want to have a look at Chloe's apartment."

"What? Why?" Honore asked. "Do you think she'd go there?"

"I checked when I left the hospital," Gennai said. "I don't have a key, so I couldn't go in, but she didn't answer when I knocked. There was no sign she'd been there recently."

I shook my head. "I want to see if there are any clues to what she might have been doing without your knowledge. We know another Practitioner who might be able to help us, too, but he needs more information about what ties Chloe might have had to the demon. And what kind of demon it might be—the areas you've tracked him in, where he frequents—" But they'd stopped listening to me.

"Another Practitioner?" Jo demanded. Her pale face had flushed with anger. "Why would you go to another Practitioner?"

"Honestly? Because I felt you were holding back on us," I said. "And as it turns out, you were. You can't expect me to help you if you don't tell me what I need to know."

"That's unacceptable," Blanche said flatly. She was frowning and her eyes had darkened. I wondered briefly at the wisdom of angering a bunch of witches. Even witches who wore Hello Kitty bandannas. "You've overstepped your bounds. We thought we could expect confidentiality from you."

"And you can. I've told the other Practitioner no names or details about you personally," I said. I was careful to say "I" because I honestly didn't know what Oliver might have told Robin; but they didn't have to know that. "Now, please tell me where the demon has been when you've successfully scried him."

Honore looked a bit sulky, but she did answer. "Almost always around clubs or bars. He seems attracted to night life."

"And it was behind a club that the murders happened," I said. "That ties in. Now, what about Chloe's apartment?"

There was silence for a minute or two. I waited them out. Finally, Honore said, "I have a key. I'll let you in."

Jo glared at her, but Honore only shrugged. "What else are we going to do? He's killed two people. If this will help..."

Trina said, "Honore is right. Stopping him has to be our top priority."

"And finding Chloe," Sasha said. Her eyes had filled with tears again.

"With luck, we'll be able to do both," I said. "What time can you meet us at Chloe's apartment?"

Honore had to go home to fetch her spare key for Chloe's apartment, so we agreed to meet at one o'clock, right after lunch. That gave me time to dither over whether to call Detective Ellis Ames and tell him our plan.

"Keep him out of it," Oliver advised. "You know we've always had better luck when we steer clear of 'official' channels."

"I know. But this time feels different," I said. "I feel like we need protection for this."

Wordlessly, Oliver held up the amulet around his neck.

I shook my head impatiently. "I'm not afraid of our clients—or at least most of them. Not so sure about Chloe at this point," I admitted. "It's the demon. I feel a lot more comfortable having a guy with a gun around if there's a possibility of running into the demon."

Oliver still looked skeptical. "Didn't seem to do much good in the hospital parking lot yesterday."

"Yeah, but the good detective didn't know what we were dealing with at that point. Now he's up to speed and he honestly seems okay with it."

"Do we even know if demons are susceptible to mundane weapons?"

"No, but we could call Robin and ask him."

Oliver pulled a deep breath and let it out. We were sitting in my office, me at my desk and Oliver in the chair opposite. He'd made coffee as soon as we came in, and we both sipped gratefully at the hot brew as we talked. "Well, it's up to you. I don't know if Honore is going to be happy to see him when we show up at the apartment, but there won't be much she can do about it at that point."

I picked up the phone. Ellis Ames answered after one ring. "Miss Sheridan? Acacia? What's up?"

"Hey, Detective," I said, making my voice casual. "We're going to check out the apartment of the witch who was in the hospital."

"Was? She's been released?"

"Not exactly. Apparently she left the hospital sometime last night—on her own, or with help. We don't know. No one's seen her since."

I heard the tick of computer keys through the phone. "She's not in the missing persons system," he told me.

"Probably hasn't been long enough yet," I said, "and I don't know how the witches are treating it.

Anyway, we're going over there to have a look around her apartment, with the permission of one of her coven sisters. Do you want to come?"

There was a pause, and then he said, "Yes, of course. Sorry. Kind of threw me there when you said, 'coven sisters.'"

"Welcome to my world. We'll be there at one o'clock; here's the address." I gave it slowly, allowing him to write it down, and then we ended the call.

"I hope you know what you're doing," Oliver said as I put my phone down.

"No more than usual."

"We're in just as much trouble as I thought we were, then. You want me to call Robin?"

"That's all right. I'll do it."

"Suit yourself." He took his coffee back to his desk.

When he'd closed the door of my office, I pulled out the little paper card with Robin's phone number on it. I was a little surprised that Oliver hadn't insisted on calling Robin himself—he still seemed touchy about Robin's involvement in the case. But maybe he was coming to terms with it.

Robin picked up on the third ring. "The Patient Frog, how may I help you?"

"Hey Robin, it's Acacia Sheridan," I said. "I have a little more information on the demon—some of it pretty bad."

"I'm sitting down already," he said, and I could hear the smile in his voice. "Let's hear it."

I told him about last night's murders and what I'd seen and felt in the vicinity. He was appropriately horrified. "The witches said that the other times they've tracked him, it's always been near clubs or bars," I added. "Do you think that's significant?"

After a pause, he said, "I do. Seems like he's drawn to the energy and vitality of night life, and no doubt the frisson of sexual energy as well."

"So, some kind of incubus?" I felt my cheeks heating up, which was ridiculous.

Robin chuckled through the phone. "Much of the traditionally accepted lore about demons is overblown and just plain wrong," he said kindly. "It's been twisted and molded to shoehorn it into various religious archetypes. Demons are, fundamentally, spirits who seek to increase their power, much as a lot of humans wish to do. They undertake it in different ways, and thus become more 'attuned,' shall we say, to different venues of acquiring that power. A demon who, loose on Earth, frequents such places is usually looking to tap into the energy of youth, vitality, and sexual vigor."

"Okay," I said slowly, "so how does knowing this help us?"

"Well, it tells you where to look for him," Robin said gently. "But it also tells you that he may come in the guise of a seducer, or he may prey upon couples for their combined energy. The fact that he killed that man and woman last night lends credence to this supposition. If you find out they were indeed romantically or sexually involved, it will be even more certain."

"Does it tell us how to fight him? What his weaknesses are?"

"To some extent, yes. Energy bonds that are not of a romantic nature will strongly counter his magic. Amulets with an air or water attunement will absorb his energy and protect you from his attacks. Fortunately, the cat's-eye you got from me will do nicely."

"Will a bullet stop him?"

There was a pause before Robin answered. "Possibly not. It could slow him down, but I wouldn't depend on it as a final answer."

"Good to know," I said, although it wasn't the answer I'd been hoping for. "The magic stuff is beyond me, but I'll pass it along to my clients, shall I?"

"Absolutely," Robin said. "And if you stop by my shop, I'll give you a couple more items I think might be particularly helpful."

"Thank you," I told him sincerely. "We'll stop by on our way to the apartment."

When we arrived at Chloe's apartment building a few minutes before one, Ellis Ames was already standing outside. It was a small block building, just four floors, with clean white and grey brick facings and what looked like a railed rooftop garden area. The landscaping was neat and conservative in a way that said it probably cost more than you'd think. It occurred to me that the market for magical beauty products must be more lucrative than I would have expected. Honore pulled up in her car as Oliver and I walked to the door, and I was suddenly struck by the contrast between this upscale building where Chloe lived, and the outdated car Honore drove. I wondered if there was really a disconnect there, and what accounted for it. Honore looked suspiciously at Ames as she approached us, so I tried to head off any trouble.

"Honore, this is Detective Ames," I said. "He's assisting with the murder investigations." I thought if I reminded her just how serious things had become, she might not protest his presence.

I guess it worked, because she simply nodded and led the way inside the building. It was just as clean and well-appointed as you might expect from the outside, with hardwood floors and the feel of an upscale hotel lobby. We took a smooth, silent elevator to the third floor, and Honore led us down a demurely-carpeted hallway. A window at the end of the corridor flooded the space with light. A table in front of the window held a large, leafy plant, and I would have laid good money that it was real. I scanned the area for any residual magical energy but found none. There were no other indications of anything amiss, either.

Honore stopped outside apartment 302 and knocked, waiting to see if there might be any response. When none came after a couple of minutes, she fitted the key into the lock and pushed the door open. "Chloe? It's Honore," she called, one last nod to the hope that her coven sister might be inside.

There was no answer.

Although it wasn't huge, Chloe's apartment had a spacious, airy feel and an open-concept layout. A double-long violet sofa dominated the living room area, offset by a couple of elegantly-carved wooden armchairs grouped conversationally across a glass-topped coffee table. One corner held a desk and computer. The white kitchen was clean and tidy, although not with the staged-for-a-magazine-shoot air of a place that didn't get used. Only two doors opened off the main kitchen/living space, so I guessed they had to be bedroom and bath. The whole place resonated with magical energy, much like the wardroom at the coven's shop. Chloe might not do magic in the hallways of her building, but she didn't hold back here.

"So, what do you want to see?" Honore asked in a flat voice. She was obviously not happy we were here, but she'd agreed to cooperate.

I turned in a circle, taking in the room. "I just want to see if there's anything here that might give us some insight into what Chloe might have been doing, or anything that might tie her to the demon. The more we know about him, the better the chance we have of finding and containing him."

Honore leaned back against the kitchen counter and crossed her arms. "Feel free," she said, but it was obvious she wasn't willing to go so far as poking around in Chole's things herself.

I turned to Oliver. "Let's just see if anything jumps out." He nodded and moved toward the computer at the other end of the room. I went to the nearest door and opened it. As I suspected, this was the bathroom, and I gave it only a cursory glance. I moved on to the bedroom.

Like the rest of the apartment, this room felt permeated with magic. The bed was a gorgeous four-poster and the room was neat and tidy. On the hardwood floor in one corner, a pentacle had been inscribed with what looked like chalk. Someone had dragged something across it, breaking the lines, although not erasing it completely.

I left it alone, but I did snap a picture on my phone to show Robin later. The tops of the night table and the dressers held nothing out of the ordinary, and although I didn't really want to, I opened each bureau drawer and gave it a quick once-over. The closet held the usual array of clothes on hangers, a few items on shelves, and a small jumble of things on the floor. Nothing of interest. I looked underneath the bed. The floor was spotless, not a dust bunny in sight. Chloe was a good housekeeper or had efficient maid service. However, a wooden box had been tucked under the head of the bed. I reached under and slid it out into the light. Sigils carved into the wooden top told me this might be a spell box—a container for all the elements of a spell, meant to lend it an enduring quality. Robin had showed me some beautiful and intricate examples in his shop and explained their purpose. Cautiously, I raised the hinged lid. Inside, a collection of small bottles nestled alongside a bundle of dried and crumbling herbs. A black wax candle showing signs of much use lay in the bottom. The bottles had been smashed, however, and the candle snapped in half.

I was about to leave the room to get Honore when I noticed that the night-table also sported a shallow drawer. I pulled it open and that oily feel of the demon's presence rolled out and hit me. The drawer held an electronic tablet like those we'd seen at Seven Sisters.

"Oliver," I called, "come in here a minute, would you?"

When he came in, I pointed to the open drawer. He glanced in and said, "Definitely feel something coming from there. And it has the same flavour as the demon."

Gingerly I reached in and picked up the device. As I turned it over to look at the back, Oliver gasped and took a step back.

Etched into the silver metal of the tablet's back were arcane symbols. Droplets of black candle wax formed small, intricate designs like the perfectly placed dots in a henna tattoo.

I glanced up sharply at Oliver. "You recognize this stuff?"

He nodded, his lips set in a firm white line. "Yes," he said bluntly. "From my previous unfortunate encounter with a witch."

His reaction had suggested as much. "What do they signify?"

"Dark magic, the kind that drains life energy from

other beings." His tone was sharp and definite.

I pressed the button to turn on the tablet and Oliver drew in a sharp breath.

"I don't think it's dangerous in my hands," I said. "I don't know anything about this stuff."

"You might be surprised," Oliver muttered, but he stood his ground.

When the tablet screen came to life, however, it was at the setup screen, as if it had been reset. I showed Oliver the spell box and the ruined pentacle.

"Maybe Chloe's been trying to reverse or undo something?"

I called to Honore to join us, and when she entered the room, Detective Ames was right behind her.

"I think the conclusion that Chloe was dabbling in dark practice is inescapable," I suggested. I showed them what I'd found.

Honore looked inside the box and then glanced at the five-pointed star inscribed on the floor. "I think you're right about the dark practice," she finally admitted. "But I did think we'd convinced her to stop."

I handed her the tablet. Honore turned it over in her hands, studying the engravings on the back. She pressed her lips into a thin line, frowning. "But the tablet has been wiped or reset. And the other things wrecked, too. Maybe that means she was done with it and had changed her mind."

"It's entirely possible," I agreed. "But maybe if she thought that was enough to break her connection to the demon, she was wrong."

"Knowing Chloe over the past couple of months, I don't think she was still trying dark practices."

I nodded. "Okay, so let's say we give Chloe the benefit of the doubt. She summoned the demon here, experimented with what he had to offer, then changed her mind. She breaks the pentacle, smashes up the stuff in the spell box, and wipes the tablet. Some time goes by. She thinks her bond with the demon has been broken, and agrees to stand as keystone again because she believes it's safe. Would that make sense?"

Honore thought about it, her brow furrowed, but eventually she nodded. "I think so. Chloe is a strong practitioner, but she's not the most particular or cautious. She tends to play the rules a bit fast and loose sometimes. She might think enough time had passed for safety without actually doing the research or counting days."

The sound of a door slamming broke the silence that fell after Honore finished speaking. I pushed past the others and ran out into the main living space, although Ames had reacted more quickly and was ahead of me. The room was empty. I crossed and pulled open the apartment door. No-one in the corridor. The elevator wasn't moving, the light glowing steadily to illuminate the number 3.

But there was a door to a stairwell at the end of the hall. I ran to it, pulled it open, and heard hasty footsteps descending the stairs. I motioned to Ames and pointed into the stairwell. He ran over and started down, making more noise than I'd hoped he would. Still, it was nice to have someone else to run after whoever had poked their nose into Chloe's apartment. I followed more quietly and heard the stairwell door at the bottom slam shut.

When I emerged into the foyer, it was empty. Ames opened the outside door and strode in, looked frustrated. He shook his head. "Whoever it was, they disappeared. I think they might have had a car waiting, maybe a taxi."

"Hmm. Or it if was the demon, he might have used magic," I said.

Ames shrugged. "Are we learning anything?"

"I think so, but let's go talk to Honore to make sure," I told him, and we climbed back up the stairs instead of waiting for the elevator.

Honore and Oliver were back in the living room, Honore still holding the tablet. I shook my head as we entered. "Whoever it was, we lost them," I said.

Oliver said, "Honore has an idea."

I grinned. "I was hoping that might be the case."

CHAPTER EIGHT

"I'll have to speak with the others first," Honore said slowly, "but I think this could work."

Not feeling comfortable making ourselves at home in Chloe's apartment—especially since we didn't know if she might have overheard us in there—we'd retired to a nearby coffee shop, The Friendly Bean, to discuss Honore's idea. Honore ordered something herbal and spicy, Oliver asked for cappuccino, Ellis Ames went with black coffee with half a sugar (to which I thought, why bother?), and I had a creamy, sweet dark coffee. We'd taken the tablet with us, Honore tucking it into her bag for safekeeping. Everything else at the apartment, we left as it had been when we arrived.

"So, what's your idea?" I asked.

Honore tapped her bag, indicating the tablet. "We use this to summon the demon. Forget having to track him down; with this, we can make him come to us."

"But I thought the tablet was wiped," Ames

protested.

Honore nodded. "It was. But we can find out what Chloe would have had installed on it for this kind of summoning—for what she was doing," she said. "The important part is that the glyphs on the back are intact. She would have put those there to single out this particular spirit. Chloe got the demon without this tablet because of their entanglement, but if we summon using the table, even without Chloe, we should get him."

"Should?" I asked, picking up on the word. "Sounds like it could be dangerous if you're wrong."

Honore lifted her chin. "I'm not wrong. And I'll consult with the others before we do anything."

"Wouldn't Chloe have known that breaking the glyphs on the back would be more important for breaking the bond to this demon than the apps or whatever on the tablet?" Oliver asked. He'd been very quiet since we'd found the tablet, but he seemed to be coming back to himself now. Seeing those glyphs had been a shock to him, I could tell.

"As I said, Chloe doesn't always do the research— she goes with her gut, or what seems right to her. I think she figured that erasing the tablet meant it couldn't be used, and if it couldn't be used, this demon had no connection to her. Especially in conjunction with wrecking the spell box and the pentacle, too. But that bond must have been a little more difficult to sever," Honore said. She turned her mug slowly around and around on the table. "I'm guessing at a lot of this, but I think I'm right."

"So if you summon him using this tablet, but do it at your wardroom, you think you'll be able to contain him long enough to get the geas in place?" I asked. Ellis Ames threw me a grateful look. I thought he must have been wanting to ask something similar but wasn't sure he had the terminology to do it.

Honore nodded slowly. "I think so. We can prepare for the arrival of a hostile entity. We just weren't expecting that the last time. There is one catch, though," she added.

I raised my eyebrows.

"What's that?" Ames asked.

"You need a seventh," Oliver said. "You're still missing Chloe, and she wouldn't be in any shape to stand in even if we could find her."

"Right," Honore said. "We'll have to reach out to the community, try to find someone willing to stand in. Not as keystone, I can do that, or maybe Jo...but yes, we need a seventh practitioner to make it work."

I opened my mouth to say that Robin might do it, then shut it again. Oliver would skin me alive if I offered up his friend without even checking with him first, and he'd be absolutely right. Honestly, Oliver might skin me alive for even suggesting that we talk to Robin about it.

Then he surprised me. "I might know someone," he said. "I can ask him—if you don't mind a male witch. I know some covens are particular about gender makeup."

Honore looked grateful. "No, that wouldn't matter to us," she said. "Is it your friend who already knows about the demon?" I got the feeling that she thought the fewer people in the Practice community who knew about their situation, the better.

Oliver nodded. "He hasn't done coven practice for quite a while—he's a bit of a lone wolf—but I can ask him." He smiled at Honore as if he hadn't been scared to death of her only a couple of short days ago. I wasn't sure what had come over him to account for the change, unless it was the fact that coming up against the dark practice he'd feared encountering had actually lightened his mental load. Sometimes once the worst fears are confirmed, then you stop worrying and start dealing.

"Now, what about Chloe?" Honore asked. She turned to Ellis Ames. "Do we need to file a formal missing persons report now? What can we do to try and find her?"

Ames looked from me to Honore. "Well, if I understand what Acacia's told me, can't you use...um...magic, to find her? Like you used to find the demon?"

Honore stared at him for a moment, then broke out into laughter. The rest of us stared at her, not getting the joke. Just when it was starting to sound a little hysterical, she quieted, shaking her head and chuckling a few times. Then she said, "Detective, thank you. We've been so preoccupied with the demon, it never occurred to me to scry for Chloe. But it's possible one of the others has thought of it and found her by now." She stood abruptly. "I should get back and find out about that. And ask them what they think of my plan."

I stood, too. "I know you don't technically need us any more to find the demon—if this works—but I feel like we should be there when you try. Just in case...well, just in case anything goes wrong. And if Oliver's friend agrees to help, that's another reason I'd like us to be present."

"Of course," Honore said. "Well, you'd have to wait in the kitchen for some of it—we wouldn't perform the entire ritual in front of non-practitioners—but we can work something out."

She looked so relieved to have a plan that I simply

said, "That's fine. I'll call you later this afternoon and see what you've decided."

She nodded, thanked us again, and left. I sank back into my chair. "Is this a good plan or a crazy one? I can't tell anymore."

Ellis Ames lifted his hands, palm out. "Don't look at me. I stopped trying to figure out what's crazy and what isn't when I realized I had to accept the existence of witches, demons, and who knows what else in my city."

Oliver pursed his lips, considering. "If Robin will go along, and if they're sure they can contain the demon, and if the summoning works the way Honore seems to think it will—"

"That's a lot of 'ifs'" I said, draining the last of my coffee.

He pulled in a deep breath and blew it out in a sigh. "It really is," he agreed, "but I do think it's a good plan."

I turned to Ames. "Why did you put her off filing a missing persons report on Chloe? I would have thought you'd want to do that by the book."

Ames shrugged. "We don't know if she's with the demon, if he got her out of the hospital, or what's happening with her. And there aren't a lot of other officers I'd feel comfortable bringing in on this, besides Crombie and Crux. They're already in, after all."

I shook my head. "They're not really 'in'," I said. "They just know there's something they don't want to be 'in', so they look the other way when it comes up."

Ames sighed. "Anyway, if the witches can find her themselves, it makes things a whole lot simpler," he said. "The hospital will be able to just let her disappearance go unexplained, if I go tell them she's been found and give them a stern talking-to about keeping better watch on the patients in their care. If the demon—or Chloe herself—used magic to get her out of there, they can't deal with that. Not stopping it or understanding it. So the more quietly we can make this all go away, the better for everyone."

I considered him. "You're an unusual cop."

"Coming from you, I think I'll take that as a compliment," he said and gave me a smile that went all the way to his eyes. "Now, can I buy us a box of doughnuts to go, and come wait at your office until we hear from Honore? I don't think I can go back to the station and face paperwork right now."

"People bearing doughnuts are always welcome at the Olympia Investigations office," I told him warmly. "Even cops. Make sure there's a lemon-filled, would you?"

The rest of the afternoon passed in a blur from there.

We ate doughnuts and drank coffee back at the office, and Oliver and I told Ellis stories of a few of our cases. He seemed genuinely interested, which was a nice change. Not that I tell many people about my work and why I do it, but the odd time I have, it hasn't always gone down well. Caro Soles is really one of the only non-supernatural beings who's accepted the strangeness of my world with equanimity. I credit her own strong cultural belief in a spirit world for her open-mindedness.

Anyway, we'd polished off most of the doughnuts and I was wondering how much exercise I'd have to do to work them off, when Honore called. Apparently, it had taken a long and not unchallenged debate, but the coven had agreed to try the summoning. They'd also scried for Chloe without success, but that could mean any number of things—including that she was dead, unconscious, or had been possessed by the demon. I decided not to dwell on those possibilities and instead believe that she was actively blocking their efforts with a concealment spell or charm, for her own inscrutable reasons.

It surprised me that Robin had agreed to help with the ritual, although admittedly I'd only just met him. I didn't know him as well as Oliver did, and Oliver seemed worried but unsurprised. When I asked him about it, Oliver sighed and said, "Robin likes to play the lone wolf as a Practitioner, but he can't stand to see anyone in trouble." It was a risky undertaking, and Robin's immediate agreement to help made me like him even more. I resolved to patronize his shop on a regular basis from now on. The summoning was set for seven o'clock that evening.

Once the doughnuts ran out, Oliver, Ellis and I ordered Chinese takeout and ate it at the office. Spending most of day there with Ellis made me realize how much the place needed a coat of paint and a general spruce-up. I realized I'd been thinking that for a long time now and putting it off. If we cleared this case tonight, I swore I was going to buy paint with some of the fee. And upon further consideration, hire a painter with some more of it. The idea of me and Oliver trying to paint the office together without killing each other defied my imagination.

With no small amount of trepidation, we arrived at Seven Sisters Health and Beauty just before seven. The shop lay mostly in darkness, with only a few ghostly night lights burning to dispel some of the gloom. Jo opened the door in answer to our knock, looking not entirely pleased but resigned. "I hope this works," she said in a slightly accusing tone, as if I'd been the one to suggest it.

"Honore seemed confident you could all make it happen, or I don't think she would have broached it to us," I said, just to clarify whose idea this had been.

She nodded and, with a slightly suspicious look at Ellis Ames, led us inside. I introduced Ellis and Jo, and she shook hands with him graciously enough. Then we followed her through to the kitchen.

Tonight, the stoves were cold and the counters clean and tidy. The bright overhead lights had been replaced by the glow from a few under-counter task lights, lending the room a restful air. Although a pleasant mix of herbs and other scents filled the space, it lacked the heady resonance of potions in mid-brew. *Even if they were only mundane beauty potions*, I thought with a smile. Then I wondered just how much magic might be infused into those products. Maybe the Seven Sisters were onto something.

Honore and Robin stood talking at the end of the kitchen, near the door leading into the wardroom. Robin's face lit up when he saw us, and he hurried over to shake Oliver's hand and give me a hug. "Oliver! Acacia! Thank you so much for being the vector that led to my meeting these wonderful compatriots! I'd almost forgotten how lovely it is to have fellow Practitioners to talk with!"

Honore gave a somewhat bemused smile, and I got

the impression that Robin had descended on the Seven Sisters like a whirlwind. I wondered how they had not been acquainted before this and made a mental note to ask Oliver about it later. This was no time for delving into Robin's personal life.

"If you three will stay in here for about ten minutes," Honore said, "then you can come through into the wardroom. We'll have the ritual well underway, so just keep back from the mandala and our circle and you'll be able to watch the proceedings."

I swallowed. "What should we expect?" I asked. "Like, when the demon appears?"

She raised her eyebrows. "Honestly, I'm not entirely sure. He may accept the geas peacefully enough, or he may try to fight it. Either way, he'll be contained inside the inner ring of the summoning circle, so there won't be any danger to you. Just don't disturb our concentration or break the circle and it should be fine. Make sure you stay *outside* the mandala once we've started," she said with emphasis.

I hoped it was as simple as that, but I still felt better having Detective Ames along. As long as he didn't freak out when the demon appeared. That could send things down a whole different road, and I didn't like the idea of travelling it.

"Any luck scrying Chloe?" I asked Honore, to get

my mind away from that troubling scenario.

Her face and shoulders sagged. "No. We tried several times, but we can't get a reading. Maybe she's out of range, or somewhere shielded."

I didn't mention the trouble they'd also had keeping a read on the demon, or ask whether the two could be related. I was sure she'd already thought of it. This wasn't the time to distract her any further.

Honore and Robin took their leave of us then, leaving us in the quiet, dimly-lit kitchen. I leaned against a counter and crossed my arms, checking the time on my watch. "Why do I feel like this is going to be a long ten minutes?"

"It's the curiosity that's killing you," Oliver said. "You're dying to know what's happening on the other side of that door."

"Well, I know I am," Ellis Ames said. "Even if I'm half-terrified to know at the same time."

I liked him better for that simple admission than for anything else he'd said since I'd known him.

We waited quietly for the rest of that ten minutes, only the slightest murmurings reaching us through the door to indicate the beginnings of the ritual. When my watch proclaimed the ten minutes were over, I squared my shoulders, pushed off the counter and said, "Shall we?" Oliver and the detective nodded, and I gingerly pushed open the wardroom door.

Inside, the room had been transformed. A multitude of candles burned inside the mandala and on the boardroom table and credenza, limning the room in a warm, buttery glow. Their combined light illuminated the mandala and the seven figures gathered around the curving circle of its outer edge, throwing a myriad of intersecting shadows across the floor and walls. The candles flickered in unison as I opened the door, even the small breath of a draft sending the flames bobbing and dancing and the shadows dancing crazily. They quickly steadied, however, as Oliver closed the door behind us.

Paler, blue-white electronic light shone from the screens of the tablets the witches held, painting their faces ghostly. None of the Practitioners wore robes or cowls or anything an overly-imaginative mind might assume for witches at a summoning—they all simply wore street clothes, which lent a much-appreciated element of normalcy to the otherworldly scene. Dotted around the room and throughout the mandala, smoldering clusters of dried herbs stood upright in colored glass vases, sending heady smoke into the air. I picked out the scents of sage, dill, and sweetgrass, but the rest was simply a morass of mixed aromas.

None of the seven, Robin or the six remaining

coven sisters, had turned to look when we opened the door and entered the room, their concentration focused on their work. A low, murmuring chant rose from all seven of the Practitioners, and if I squinted, I could discern a dim, greenish glow surrounding each tablet. This bore no relation to the light from the screen—it must be a manifestation of the spell energy being drawn from the power of the online world. *Cat videos*, I thought with an inner smile. I was distracted from that thought almost immediately, though, as the inner circle of the mandala began to glow with a pulsing amber light. A mist shimmered above it and I realized it must be the demon, beginning to take form. I took an involuntary step backward and felt someone grasp my hand. I looked over and saw that it was Ellis Ames. His eyes were fixed on the coalescing mist, but his fingers tightened around mine.

I thought I understood. His understanding of the world had been challenged in the last few days, and what he'd accepted in the abstract, he was about to witness in reality. Anyone might want a hand to hold at a moment like that.

And then the door to the kitchen flew open and a wild-eyed, wind-blown Chloe screamed, "What the hell are you doing?"

CHAPTER NINE

The candle flames fluttered in the sudden change of air, shadows diving and pitching around the room again. Some of the candles guttered out. The lazy, upward-drifting streams of smoke from the smoldering herbs shuddered and fragmented, embers flaring like baleful orange eyes in the dim light. The coalescing mist of the demon spirit trembled and convulsed.

To their credit, none of the witches panicked. Tablet screens twitched, sending shadows dancing weirdly over faces, but the chanting voices faltered only slightly before rebounding. That was good, because as I found out later, Chloe made her entrance at the most sensitive part of the summoning—when the demon was partially formed. Whether they knew they couldn't afford to let go of their concentration or they trusted the remaining three of us to contain Chloe, I didn't know.

"Contain Chloe" was precisely what Ellis Ames and

I thought, however. After an initial moment of shock, he and I both started for the doorway where she stood. Even in the dim light of the wardroom and the kitchen behind her, it was evident that Chloe was not in the best of shape. She'd ditched her hospital gown somewhere and wore a pair of torn black tights and an oversized fisherman's sweater. Her feet were shoved into scuffed ballet flats that looked a little too big for her. Her blonde hair had been caught back at the nape of her neck, but still looked sweat-damp. Much of it had come loose and dangled wildly at the sides of her face. The bandages remained on her left hand and forehead, but now they were dirty and straggling.

All this I took in at a glance, but it was her eyes that took most of my attention. They were wild and frantic, the whites showing like those of a frightened horse.

But she wasn't frenzied enough to miss our presence. As soon as Ellis moved in her direction, she sprinted into the room, circling away from us around the mandala and the ring of witches. She must know we wouldn't risk breaking the circle. I heard her voice rise above the coven's steady chant, intoning words that sounded all too familiar to me. They sounded suspiciously like the beginning of the spell she'd cast in the hospital. We had to stop her, and fast. But we couldn't chase her around and around the huge mandala like characters in a cartoon.

"Go that way!" I hissed to Ellis, pointing after Chloe. I ran around the circle in the other direction, figuring if we split her attention and came at her from two sides, we'd catch her between us in the middle. He got the idea right away and went after her.

Chloe was too crafty for us, though. She didn't stop on the other side of the circle but sprinted all the way to the far end of the room. She turned, put her back to the wall, and shot a hand out toward Ellis Ames.

"Down!" I called, remembering the explosion Oliver and I had heard come from the hospital room. Whatever Chloe was about to throw at Ames, it wouldn't be good.

I like a man who listens. Ellis threw himself sideways and down, sliding across the polished floor to bump into one of the credenza's legs. A flash of light blossomed where Ellis had been seconds before, and bits of concrete shrapnel peppered up from the point where Chloe's magical energy impacted the floor.

I slowed and ducked, covering my face instinctively although the shrapnel probably wouldn't reach this far. Unfortunately, my reaction gave Chloe the time to cast another spell. This one was quick; I heard a single, low-voiced word slither over my hearing and felt a tug in my chest as if someone had tied a string around my heart and jerked it. I gasped and staggered, going down on one knee. I heard Ellis grunt as if someone had gut-punched him.

Chloe. I had to reach her. The string around my heart had vanished after that single yank, and I gasped, trying to fill my lungs. Somehow, I got to my feet, staggered, then ran. I ran straight at Chloe and lunged for her. With her back against the wall, she had nowhere to go, and we landed on the floor in a tumble. My elbow hit the wall and I felt a flash of pain and then numbness. Chloe's scream of rage split the air and almost deafened me since I was so close to her face. She fought like a wildcat then, scratching and struggling and swearing at me in French.

I grappled with her flailing arms, wondering where he hell Ellis was. Surely he'd had time to get to his feet and come help me?

Then I felt it. Or rather, I smelled it first—the dark, oily scent I now associated with the demon. On the heels of the scent came a chill that struck to my bones, and a wash of omnipresent, lowering darkness. I assumed this meant the demon had fully arrived, but I hadn't expected his presence to be so overwhelming— not when he was confined within the mandala's containing circle. Maybe Ellis had been overcome by the sensation, I thought raggedly as I tried to keep

Chloe's clutching hands from reaching my face. If that was the case, I needed him to snap out of it and come help me.

"Ellis!" I managed to yell. "Detective Ames!"

There was no answer.

Then Chloe stopped fighting me, jerked once and went limp. I fell across her as she collapsed, then pushed myself up to look around. The room had darkened; most of the candles had been extinguished, and most of the blue-white light from the tablet screens was gone, too. The silence hit me. The witches had ceased their low chanting. That felt wrong. Wrong, and dangerous. Squinting, I pushed myself away from Chloe and tried to see into the mandala.

Something dim and red pulsed at the centre, and I realized it was the floor of the mandala's central circle. It glowed as if red-hot, but the figure standing in it didn't seem to find it warm. A faint green glow encircled the red, though—the outer perimeter of the containment circle. For now, at least, the witches' power held. A voice slid around the room, like a snake's tongue tasting the air for prey. It wasn't a harsh voice, but it grated across my eardrums with a sickening pressure.

"*Thank you for inviting me,*" it said. "*This seems...intriguing.*"

That's when I made sense of the *wrongness* of the scene before me. Where there should have been seven standing figures with the demon in the centre, I could make out only three upright bodies. Something cold clutched at my gut. *Where was Oliver? And what had happened to the others?*

Ellis Ames slid up next to me in the darkness. His breath sounded harsh and fast, but he kept his voice to a whisper as he asked the same thing. "Where is everybody?"

"I don't know. But we need to find out." I thought of something. I slipped Oliver's protective ring off my thumb and passed it to Ellis. "Put this on."

He let me press it into his palm, but asked, "What is it?"

"Protection," I said tersely. "Just put it on."

"What about you?"

"I have more," I said, touching the amulet still around my neck, under my shirt. "Put the damn thing on." He didn't argue again, so I assumed he'd done as I asked. Staying low, I crab-walked slowly toward the mandala and the space where, if I remembered correctly and hadn't gotten completely disoriented by the darkness, Blanche should have been standing.

I saw the light of her tablet first, a faintly-glowing rectangle outlined on the floor. The device lay face-down, the uneven surface of the mosaic tiles allowing light from the screen to creep out around the sides. As I got closer, I saw the outline of a limp hand limned by that light.

A woman's halting voice began to pick up the chant again—Honore, I thought. Robin's voice joined her from across the circle, and then one I thought was Jo. Thank goodness. They were getting things back on track. Maybe Ellis and Oliver and I could figure out help the others. I put a hand out, reaching tentatively to touch Blanche's arm. Her skin felt warm, but she didn't respond. I shook her arm.

"*A geas?*" came the oily voice again, the one I knew was the demon. "*Oh, I don't think so, little mice.*"

From where the demon stood, a wave of purple light washed out, expanding like ripples on a pond. When it reached me, I had the sudden sensation of a thousand spiders crawling over my skin. A momentary pressure constricted my heart and beat against my eyeballs and eardrums. Behind me, I heard Ellis draw in a sharp breath. The feeling passed as quickly as it had come, though. Across the mandala from me, I saw the purple light flow over and around Robin, but it didn't seem to touch him. Honore, Robin and Jo continued to chant.

"What was that?" Ellis whispered.

I shrugged, although I knew he couldn't see me well in the dark. "Some kind of spell," I said, "but I think he's weak as long as he stays contained in the circle. My amulet and that ring I gave you probably protected us, too." I knew Oliver had his own protections, but I was worried about him. *Where was he?* The witches must have had their own protections. They hadn't all worked against whatever had laid more than half of them low, however. That spell Chloe had cast? The timing seemed right. Whatever. I didn't have to understand what had happened. We had to get them conscious and up. I leaned forward to find Blanche's shoulders and give her another shake, but Ellis laid a hand on my arm.

"They said don't break the circle," he said. "Stay outside the mandala. I guess that still counts, right?"

Damn. He was right. I had leaned into the circle, but I hadn't touched down inside it. Nothing bad had seemed to happen, so I figured I hadn't crossed the line. "Okay, just help me drag her closer to us. We don't touch inside, and we don't move her outside the perimeter."

Beside me, Ellis nodded, and together we edged Blanche closer. I ran my hands over her head and face, but I couldn't feel any injury. The pulse in her neck beat strong and regular under my fingertips. "I think she's just unconscious," I said. I tapped lightly on the woman's cheeks, but she didn't respond. I gave her what might be construed as a slap, but still nothing. It didn't seem wise to assault a sleeping witch any further than that.

"Maybe someone else," Ellis suggested.

We started to half-crawl around the circle when red light flashed in the centre and the demon's voice came again. This time it sounded less amused. An edge of frustration leaked through his words. *I will not be contained, nor bound. You are too weak to hold me, and I have...tasted the pleasures of this world.*

Honore, Robin, and Jo kept up their chant, but I knew without the other four witches there was probably no hope of setting the geas on the demon. It was up to me, Ellis, and Oliver to get the other women on their feet. I just wasn't sure how to do that.

The central ring flared a brighter red for a moment, then faded again. The green light around it pulsed and then steadied. The demon was testing the strength of his bonds. The three witches' voices faltered out of step for a word or two, then re-harmonized.

"Forget the others for now," I hissed to Ellis. "I have to talk to Oliver."

I hoped to find Oliver working on waking the sleepers, but instead I found him pretty much exactly where I'd left him. He slumped against the wall near the door to the kitchen. In the unsteady light of a single candle still burning nearby, I could see his eyes were closed, his hands clenched into fists at his sides. His breath came in short pants. I touched his arm and he flinched. "Oliver," I whispered, "what is it?"

He shook his head a little. "Chloe," he croaked. "She pulled—did you feel—"

I squeezed his arm and nodded. "I did. But only a little, right? Robin's protections worked. She pulled some energy from us, but not much. We're okay."

He breathed deeply and exhaled, then nodded, eyes still squeezed shut as if he could hide. "I don't know what's happening."

"Four of the witches are down," I said. "Maybe from Chloe's spell, I don't know. But we have to wake them up somehow."

"Without breaking the circle," Ellis added. That instruction had certainly made an impression on him.

"What did she do to them?" Oliver asked.

I shook my head. "I don't know. They seem fine, just asleep. We need to wake them," I repeated.

A low growl filled the room, and I turned to see the mandala's centre pulse a brighter red again. This time the green light retreated, almost fading out before it flared back. We were running out of time.

Oliver opened his eyes suddenly and grasped my arm, pulling me toward the kitchen door. I thought he was trying to leave, so I pulled back. "We can't leave Robin and—"

He shook his head impatiently. "We need something in there," he hissed, and pulled again. This time I let him take me into the kitchen, Ellis close on our heels.

As soon as the door closed behind us, Oliver said, "Peppermint oil—they've got to have some here. Smelling salts would be better, but peppermint is strong. It might wake them."

"Worth a try," I said, and the three of us rummaged through the cupboards. Oliver finally found a small bottle marked *Peppermint* and unstoppered it, dropping some of the oil on two wads of paper towel and handing one to each of us. Quietly, and opening the door as narrowly as possible, we slipped back into the near-dark room and split up, moving out around the mandala.

I wasn't sure which of the witches was closest to me—Trina, I thought as I knelt near her, careful not to cross the boundary of the circle. The meagre candle light glinted off her many piercings. Fortunately, she had fallen close to the mandala's edge, and I only had to turn her head a little toward me. I put the minty toweling under her nose and willed it to work.

After a couple of breaths, it did. Trina jerked and flinched her face away, one arm flailing out and almost hitting me in the face. I leaned close and whispered, "You have to get up and resume the spell. They need you."

After a couple more disoriented seconds, she seemed to grasp what I was saying. She sat up, feeling around for her tablet, but she couldn't find it.

"Never mind," she said finally. "This is wasting time. I'll draw on my own energy." She got shakily to her feet and took up the chant along with the others. Her voice was weak, but it strengthened as it joined the others.

I heard another voice return to the chorus. Red flared at the axis of the mandala again, and this time a bright wall leapt like flames around the demon. He growled again, louder this time, a sound so furious and primal that a knot like cold iron formed in my gut. I edged around to where I knew Blanche lay and thrust the peppermint-soaked paper under her nose. She sputtered and coughed. "Blanche," I whispered, "you have to wake up."

Like Trina, she came around quickly and grasped the situation. She found her tablet, still glowing, and put out a hand for me to help her up, already beginning to mouth the words of the chant as she found her way in. The demon pushed against the boundaries of the inner circle again, red light flaring as he did so, but this time the encircling green was brighter with the power of the revived coven sisters. We were almost back to full strength, and he must have known that he wouldn't be able to hold out against the full coven.

Then a shriek of hysterical laughter cut through the chant, and my heart went cold.

We'd forgotten about Chloe.

CHAPTER TEN

This time, Chloe didn't waste time with spells. She bolted straight past me and into the mandala.

If I hadn't been still helping to steady Blanche, I might have realized what Chloe was doing in time to stop her. As it was, I stood dumbly as she darted directly to her demon.

And all hell literally broke loose.

When Chloe broke the circle, the witches' chant cut off as if it had been guillotined. Crimson light blossomed out from the central rings like an eerie red tide, illuminating Chloe where she had come to rest, with her arms wrapped around the figure of the demon. He raised a hand and caressed her hair, its pale blonde now limned by a hellish red glow. I stared in horror at that hand, as the realization struck home that this was the demon without his illusory veneer of humanity, as we'd seen at the hospital. Now the fingers stroking Chloe's hair were elongated and knobby, with long, cruel-looking claws.

"Shit," Blanche said succinctly. "We have to get back."

Half-dragging the witch, I backed up to the wall near the kitchen door. Oliver and Gennai were already there. Without any apparent consultation, the two witches began a new spell, one I hoped would be protective. I peered into the fiendish light searching for Ellis, but there were too many moving shadows to pick him out.

"Well, this is stupid," Oliver muttered, and smacked his palm on the wall. He'd obviously noticed a light switch, because the overhead lights sprang to life, illuminating the room with pale, cool fluorescence. Startled faces turned to us, then almost as one, turned back to the demon.

The light was a mixed blessing. It robbed the situation of a certain amount of creepiness and let us see where everyone was and what shape they were in.

Unfortunately, it also let us see the demon.

He towered a good two feet over Chloe, which I'd been able to see even before Oliver hit the lights. However, I hadn't had such a good look at the taut, leathery skin of his face, or the way his lips didn't seem quite big enough to cover the hideous-looking teeth filling his mouth. I hadn't been able to make out the yellow irises of his eyes as they darted around the room with a malevolent glare.

And honestly, I hadn't needed to see that.

Ellis backed up to the wall near us. He had his gun in his hand, but Sasha, whom he'd helped over, snapped, "Put it away, Detective. It won't do much good against him and you might hurt one of us." She turned from him and joined Blanche and Gennai in their spell-weaving.

He turned wide eyes toward me. "A gun won't hurt him?"

I shrugged. "They're the experts," I said. "I'd believe them."

Muttering, he stuck it back in his holster. "Now what?"

As if in answer, a shimmer appeared in the air in front of us. Glancing sideways, I saw that Robin had backed a few feet away from the mandala, and had pulled an odd-looking stick from somewhere—he hadn't had it before, not that I'd seen. He held it pointing down at the floor, and now a slightly iridescent, lustrous wall separated us from the demon. Only those of us on this side of the room, unfortunately; me, Oliver and Ellis, Blanche, Sasha, Gennai, and Robin himself. Honore, Jo, and Trina, on the opposite side of the mandala when Chloe broke the circle, had backed to the far wall.

Apparently intrigued, the demon left the inner circle—with the boundary of the mandala breached and the witches' spell disrupted, nothing contained him there any longer. Chloe stumbled a bit as he broke away from her, and I heard Honore call her name. Chloe appeared not to hear her, following the demon. He strode to the shimmering wall, the claws on his feet *ticking* incongruously across the mosaic tiles. He reached out a finger to touch the wall. Where the claw made contact, electricity sparked and he drew back. The corners of his lips pulled up in a smile that was more of a grimace, considering that mouthful of teeth.

"You'll keep," he hissed, then turned and threw a roil of dark energy across the room toward Honore, Jo and Trina. I saw it catch Chloe and knock her back a few steps, but the demon didn't seem to notice—or care.

Jo had done something similar to Robin's wall, however. She held a small disc out toward the demon's attack, and the dark energy funneled into it, whirlpooling into the disc before it could reach the witches.

The demon threw back his head and laughed. "*Use all the tricks you have,*" he rasped finally. "*You'll run out eventually.*" Then his eyes fell on Chloe, and he tilted his head at her, considering. He grinned evilly. *"On second thought, maybe I don't want to wait."*

I heard Robin's indrawn breath, almost a gasp. He must have known what the demon intended, but it happened too fast for him to do anything—if there was anything he could have done. The creature took two steps toward Chloe and caught her in the crook of his left arm. He spoke a single, guttural word in a language I didn't recognize, then slashed her right arm open with one swipe of a hooked claw. Blood blossomed from the wound.

I know I yelped in surprise and horror, but it was drowned out by the screams of Chloe's coven sisters. After a confused few seconds, though, I realized they weren't screaming in horror, as I was—they were screaming in pain. Every woman had gasped her own right arm, shrieking as if they, too, had felt the demon's claw slice their skin. Trina had gone to her knees, and Gennai fell against the wall beside me. I turned to help her, but I felt a hand on my shoulder. I turned and saw Robin, his face grave. At least he'd been unaffected by the demon's action.

"Acacia," he said in an urgent voice. "I need you. We only have once chance."

"What did he do to them?" My voice sounded very small, even to me.

"Tapped into their vulnerability—Chloe's connection to the coven," he said. "I didn't know—look, I'll explain later. We don't have time."

I nodded, tried to snap myself out of my stupor. The demon advanced toward the other three witches, dragging Chloe with him. Blood dripped off her dangling arm, leaving a horrible trail across the mandala. She appeared to have fallen into unconsciousness.

"You have your amulet?" Robin asked me.

I nodded.

"Oliver's okay...what about him?" He nodded toward Ellis Ames.

"He's got a ring...the one you gave Oliver earlier," I said.

Robin nodded once. "They'll do. Will you help me power a spell?"

"Um—sure, I guess. What do I have to do?"

"Get the detective's permission, too. I must have a word with Oliver. Try to distract the demon for a minute."

"I—what?" But Robin had bent toward Oliver, talking low and urgently. Oliver looked pale.

I turned to Ellis. "He said we have to distract the demon."

I felt sorry for the poor detective in that moment.

He'd been so willing to accept everything I'd told him about this world he'd been so blissfully unaware of before this case, and I knew he was really trying. But the past few minutes had stretched his aplomb to the breaking point and beyond. He gaped at me.

"We have to distract the demon," I said, louder.

His eyes looked a little glazed. Still handsome, but it was like someone had switched the light off behind them. "Detective!" I shouted. "Ellis!" And I reached up and slapped him.

I'd held back when I was trying to wake Blanche, but I didn't now. My hand stung from the impact. But it worked. Ellis' eyes cleared. He pulled his gun again.

"You think this will do it? Even if it won't hurt him?"

"Give it a try. Robin said a bullet might slow him down." With luck, even a demon couldn't entirely ignore being shot in the back. "Oh, and will you help power a spell for Robin?"

"Whatever, sure. I just want to get the hell out of here." Ellis took aim and pulled the trigger. The sound echoed around the room and I instinctively put my hands over my ears. I saw the demon jerk and stumble forward, so at least it should get his attention.

It did. He turned with a snarl and dropped Chloe. Claws out, he lunged toward us. The shimmer wall was still there, but I wasn't sure I trusted it to hold back this charge. I didn't want to watch it fail.

Luckily, I didn't have to. Suddenly Oliver was there, putting an arm around my shoulders and one around Ellis'. "This is going to hurt a little," he said. "Just brace yourselves, okay? Take my hand."

"What do you—" I started, but that was as far as I got. I heard Robin intone a few words in that otherworldly language, and then the amulet around my neck buzzed against my skin like a phone on vibrate.

"Hold hands," Oliver ground out between clenched teeth, and I felt his fingers twine through mine. Ellis reached over and took my other one, and we formed a circle of three. I felt pitifully unequal to the task that even the seven witches hadn't managed.

Then the pull hit me. This time it wasn't just on my heart. The strings had been tied around my brain, my heart, my gut, and Robin was tugging on them all at once. I blinked and shook my head, but Oliver squeezed my hand tighter. "Try...to...relax," he managed. Ellis Ames groaned and I thought he might break my fingers, he was clutching them so hard.

But beside us, Robin was still talking. He'd dropped the stick—or wand—he'd held earlier, and now a glass sphere about the size of a golf ball rested in the palm of one outstretched hand. Miniature bolts of multicoloured lightning crackled inside it, and the entire sphere glowed with an azure aura. As the sphere brightened, I felt the pull on my energy strengthen. My legs began to tremble and I tried to lock my knees. I wondered how long I could stay upright as the strength drained out of me.

The demon roared. Out of the corner of my eye I saw him impact our protective wall. It sparked and hissed, undulating but holding. Robin raised his voice and the sphere higher. The demon blasted a torrent of dark energy toward us and the barrier held, stretched...and buckled. The wave rushed over us like roiling smoke and my amulet went cold, biting icy fingers into my flesh. When the cloud cleared, though, I felt like it had barely touched me. Ellis and Oliver looked shaken but still standing, although Ellis had half-collapsed against the wall behind him. My hands were slick with sweat and I fought to keep our circle unbroken.

The demon reached for the sphere in Robin's hand and I imagined him crushing it like an egg. But Robin spoke a final, reverberating word that crashed up against my eardrums and left them ringing. A final pull of energy felt like I was turning inside-out and I gasped aloud, dropping to one knee.

Then the sphere's azure glow brightened to

blinding, and I squeezed my eyes shut against the light. The demon screamed once, a sound reverberating with hate, and then it cut off abruptly. The pull released at the same time, as if all those strings had been cut with one swipe of a knife. Oliver and I sagged next to Ellis, panting. I heard a thump. Robin had collapsed. I half-crawled to him and put a hand on his head. He didn't open his eyes, but the corners of his mouth pulled up in a smile.

He croaked, "We did it."

The sphere lay beside him on the floor, its azure glow extinguished. Inside the glass, a dark blot swirled and circled as if trying to get out. I didn't even want to know the explanation for that.

I put one hand on my chest, where my heart beat heavy and slow as if it had settled to the very bottom of my ribcage. Oliver dragged himself across the floor to join us. Beyond him, Ellis lay on his back, breathing heavily. Oliver looked as ragged as I'd ever seen him, but maybe a little triumphant, too.

"I never, ever want to do that again," I told him.

"I warned you about witches," he croaked, and collapsed next to Robin.

EPILOGUE

A week later, I sat back in my desk chair and sipped coffee, enjoying the simple pleasure of the spreading warmth as I swallowed. I'd given Oliver a few well-deserved days off, and the office was quiet. I'd just hung up the phone from talking to Honore Martel. The coven had paid my fee in full and added something extra to acknowledge that maybe Oliver and I had gone beyond the call of duty. Chloe had landed back in the hospital, but they'd stitched her up. With the demon gone, she'd come back to herself, asserting that the demon had been controlling her ever since the fateful summoning-gone-wrong. On the questions of whether the others believed her, and whether she would continue as one of the Seven Sisters, Honore hadn't given me a straight answer, and I didn't press her. The coven would have to work those things out for themselves.

Robin, too, had needed a couple of days in the hospital, but he was home again and tending to his shop. I stopped by to check on him the day he was released, and we had tea together. He told me some things that gave me pause.

"That's what happened to Oliver when he was younger, wasn't it?" I asked as we shared an entire half of a fresh-baked apple pie. With my mouth full of flaky pastry and tangy-sweet apple, I didn't feel the slightest twinge of guilt. "A witch used his life energy to power spells. But not with his consent."

Robin nodded gravely. "And without the protective items you all had. That would have made it far worse. It's a terrible thing to do to someone, even in the circumstances of the other night," he said, frowning. "Believe me, Acacia, I didn't enjoy doing that. But I couldn't see any other way."

I took another heavenly bite of pie and chewed slowly, following it with a sip of sweet tea. "I wouldn't want to do it again," I said. "But it worked. The demon's gone, and no-one else died. We're all okay. It was worth it."

"Demons are a lot of trouble," Robin observed. "I hope that's the last one I ever encounter."

"You and me, both," I agreed. I almost said something to the effect that I hoped I was through with witches, too, then remembered who had served me this amazing pie. There were witches, and then there were witches. The ones like Robin brought more than toil and trouble.

"I'm glad Oliver had you to talk to about his experience," I said. "He's never told me any details beyond what I pieced together myself."

Robin chuckled. "He's never told me much, either. I think he keeps those details close to his chest. I wish he *would* talk to someone about them. It would probably be healthier."

I frowned. "Then how did you know? About what happened to him?"

"Who do you think put a stop to the witch who was using him?" Robin asked with a rueful smile.

But he wouldn't say anything more about it.

The phone rang in my office again, jolting me out of my reverie. I let go of the memory of the pie with some regret and picked up.

Ellis Ames said, "Hey, how are you? Still recovering?"

"I'm doing pretty well," I said, "How about you?"

I heard the smile in his voice. "Apart from having to convince myself every morning that it was real and I didn't just dream it, I'm fine."

"Crombie and Crux give you the third degree?"

He chuckled. "You were right. Those two are much happier not knowing the details. They know it, and now

I know it. So, we have an understanding."

"What about the higher-ups? They're never going to clear those two murders off the books."

"I know." He sighed. "But your friend Dr. Lewis has them convinced that there's no useful forensic evidence, so I guess it will go into the cold case file. No comfort for their families, though."

"They wouldn't be any happier if they knew the truth."

"I think you're right." He was quiet for a moment, then said, "On a brighter note, would you have any interest in going out for coffee on the weekend?" His voice was casual, but there was an undertone of seriousness. "I...don't have anyone else to talk things over with, and I feel like I still need to."

"Um...sure," I said. I liked Ellis Ames and his warm grey eyes. I hoped he wasn't just using me as a therapist while he came to terms with the existence of witches, demons, and other supernatural elements in his otherwise mundane world. But I could stand to drink some coffee while we figured that out.

I found myself smiling. Maybe the witches had brought me more than toil and trouble after all.

THE END

About the Author

Sherry D. Ramsey is a speculative fiction writer, editor, publisher, creativity addict and self-confessed internet geek. When she's not writing, she makes jewelry, gardens, hones her creative procrastination skills on social media, and consumes far more coffee and chocolate than is likely good for her.

Sherry writes for both adults and younger readers. Her books include three books in the Nearspace series, *One's Aspect to the Sun, Dark Beneath the Moon,* and *Beyond the Sentinel Stars;* the urban fantasy *The Murder Prophet;* two books for middle-grade readers, *The Seventh Crow* and *Planet Fleep*; and two collections of short stories. *Toil and Trouble* is the fourth Olympia Investigations tale.

With her partners at Third Person Press (http://www.thirdpersonpress.com) she has co-edited six anthologies of regional short fiction. Every November she disappears into the strange realm of National Novel Writing Month and emerges gasping at the end, clutching something resembling a novel.

A member of the Writer's Federation of Nova Scotia Writer's Council, Sherry is also a past Vice-President and Secretary-Treasurer of SF Canada,

Canada's national association for Speculative Fiction Professionals.

You can visit Sherry online at her website, www.sherrydramsey.com, to find free stories and more, check Facebook for Sherry D. Ramsey Writing News, and follow her on Twitter or Instagram @sdramsey. She also pins some fun things (including a series of visual writing prompts) on Pinterest – just look for Sherry D. Ramsey.

Sign up for her monthly newsletter at www.sherrydramsey.com to receive a free book, and get all the latest news on releases, giveaways, contests, and more.

The *Olympia Investigations* Series
Multiformat ebooks – visit
www.sherrydramsey.com to learn more